THE BRITTLER SISTERS
BOOK THREE

Charlotte

USA TODAY BESTSELLING AUTHOR

JOSEPHINE BLAKE

Chapter One

———❖———

She couldn't breathe. Charlotte held onto the bedpost for dear life as her mother cinched her stays even tighter than she had the day before.

"There," she said, at last, tying off the ends and stepping back to admire the effect she had created. "You look perfect. Where's your gown?"

"Mother," gasped Charlotte, turning on the spot to face the woman with her hand pressed to her ribs. "I'll be passed out in the middle of the dance floor within the hour. My toes are tingling."

"Tosh," said Samantha Brittler. She waved her hand dismissively and moved to the wardrobe. Charlotte glared at her, already feeling light-headed.

"I'm quite serious, Mother," grumbled Charlotte as she tottered over to the dressing table and began running her fingers through the rigidly fashionable curls her mother had wound about her head. "I won't be dancing at all if you insist I go like this."

Samantha ignored her. She was good at that. "This one will do perfectly," she said, removing a blue silk gown from the wardrobe and laying it out on the bed. Charlotte sighed.

"Slide that on at once. I'll send for Penny in a moment to help do up the buttons."

Charlotte frowned after her mother as she exited the room, then she listened to her enter her sister's room next door.

Her chest was already heaving as she struggled to take in enough tiny puffs of air to keep her body functioning.

"This is ridiculous," she muttered to herself, eyeing her reflection. Her waist was pulled in so tightly that she could encircle it with her hands and her elegant fingers would touch on both ends. Her long red hair dangled down her back as she turned in the mirror to gaze at the laces of her stays. Her fingers were white and bloodless. She gasped and began fumbling with the ties behind her back.

She heard the bedroom door open and her hands dropped to her sides as she looked up to see who had entered. Noelle slunk into the room, looking quite as uncomfortable as Charlotte.

"I'll loosen yours if you loosen mine," she whispered.

Charlotte smiled in relief and waved her sister over to her, hardly having the breath left to speak.

Noelle let out a tiny gasp as Charlotte worked her fingers expertly over her sister's laces. They fell loose at once, and Noelle's face flooded with color.

"She's been so much worse since Di left," she said, turning around and nudging Charlotte's shoulder, still breathing like a wounded horse. Charlotte spun her back to her sister and held her breath so that Noelle would have room to maneuver the strings.

At last, they came free, and she sucked in great lungfuls of air while her head spun dizzily. Charlotte made her way over to the bed and collapsed next to her blue dress. Noelle followed her.

"She's worried," said Charlotte, rubbing her temples and gazing at the face of her wardrobe without seeing it. "She thinks if she doesn't get us married off, we'll leave her, like Di."

"Dianna didn't abandon us," said Noelle, a dreamy look coming over her face. "She left to find love." Charlotte snorted and Noelle glared at her. "She did!" she insisted.

"We haven't heard from her in weeks, 'Elle."

"She said she would write when she came into town. She said Greyson was very pleasant, but that she wouldn't be able to write much," Noelle quoted stubbornly.

"She's glossing it over. You know as well as I do Dianna was searching for an adventure. She'd be happy with or without this man."

"They're going to fall in love," muttered Noelle. "Just you wait."

Charlotte rolled her eyes as her sister headed for the door and opened it a crack. She peered out into the hallway beyond and then looked back over her shoulder.

"Mother's in Sarah's room."

"You go in and rescue her once mother sends for Penny."

Noelle nodded to show she understood and then slithered back through the door, closing it softly behind her.

A few moments later, Charlotte heard a bell ring in the downstairs kitchen. Penny, the housemaid, entered her room.

"She's got you trussed up like a thanksgiving turkey, she has," giggled the girl as she deftly tugged Charlotte's gown onto her shoulders and began buttoning the back of the bodice. "How are your stays?"

"Noelle loosened them a bit," responded Charlotte with a grimace. Penny nodded and moved out of the room. Charlotte was left alone with nothing to distract her but her very irritable thoughts. She listened to the sounds of her mother readying her sisters for the night's event and a spark of anger lit in her chest.

It was a few moments before she realized what had infuriated her. Dianna. Stubborn, wonderful Dianna. Her eldest sister. If only she were here, she would be able to calm their mother's anxieties.

Thomas and Samantha Brittler had four daughters. Four, stubborn, idealistic daughters with enough will to flatten a mountain range. Dianna had been the first, and so, she was also the first to go. She had left them. Quite of her own volition.

Left her mother and father and three sisters behind in Manhattan to travel across the country and marry a man she had never met. Well. Noelle might find that romantic. She, Charlotte, found it tasteless. And though she would rather bite off her tongue than admit it, a small part of her agreed with their mother's blatant opinion on the matter.

Of course, she knew why Dianna had left them. She knew it as surely as she knew that the sun would come in the morning. Dianna had left, not out of selfishness or spite, but out of need.

Charlotte understood that Dianna had needed something more. She'd never been happy with their way of living. With the day-to-day calls and charity work and sewing. She had wanted to live, and Charlotte couldn't blame her, but it didn't stop her being angry with her.

Dianna was the only one of the four girls who could ever manage to curb their mother's overzealous nature. Samantha Brittler was a former debutante with a taste for the social aspect of Manhattan. She liked to see and be seen, and she did not approve of Dianna's decision to travel westward, not in the slightest. Dianna had been the only one of the Brittler sisters with enough of Samantha's own genes to contradict her ridiculousness.

She had been logical, to the point of being irritating, but then there were times when some whim or feeling had taken hold of her and she would throw her logic to the wind. Her personality was a kaleidoscope of contradictions. Next to her eldest sister, Charlotte always felt robustly sane. She knew what she wanted, and she knew how to get it. She did it quietly and without fuss. If Dianna had been logical, but reckless, Charlotte was clever and fierce. She liked that about herself. She liked the ability to see past dreams and frivolities. She did not ache for change. No. If she could only find a husband, she would be content with life in Manhattan. Or in some closely related facsimile.

A husband who would care for her, and most importantly, love her. She'd seen examples of loveless marriages. She'd had friends who had been matched with wealthy men so that their families could profit. They were lonely.

If Charlotte was sure about anything, she was sure about this. She would marry one day, and she would marry for love. She wouldn't take a chance on a stranger. No. She would love the man she married, and she would be absolutely certain that he loved her in return.

A knock sounded on her bedroom door once more and her mother entered without waiting for a response.

"Are you ready?"

Charlotte stood up. She was within an inch of her mother's height, but while Samantha was slender, Charlotte's silhouette was full of curves. She was shapely, with long legs. Her waist dipped in pleasantly, and her long red hair was rich and thick in texture.

She looked very little like the rest of her family. It wasn't just her brilliantly red hair, it was in her facial structure, and in the way she moved and talked. She was different.

"I just need my necklace," she said dispassionately. She retrieved it from her vanity and allowed her mother to fasten it about her neck.

"There," said Samantha, bestowing a rare smile on her. "You look lovely. Let's be off then."

Charlotte rode in the carriage next to the window. It was another dreary Manhattan evening. Their weather had been abysmal as of late. Noelle and Sarah chatted amicably, but Charlotte couldn't even muster the energy to feign interest in their conversation.

"How do you think he'll do it?" asked Noelle from the other side of the carriage.

"I don't even know that he will, 'Elle," giggled Sarah. She blushed.

"You do too. He's absolutely smitten with you. He's bound to ask you to marry him."

Samantha Brittler cast Sarah-Jane an approving look. Sarah had recently managed to capture the attention of Fredrick Carson Williamson. The son of a wealthy coal merchant from England, whose father their mother had been acquainted with in childhood. Carson had traveled to America on business and now seemed quite taken with Sarah. Their mother could not have been more pleased to make the introduction, or to take the credit for their running courtship.

"He's wonderful, isn't he?" sighed Sarah, her breath steaming against the window. Her eyes were wide and dreamy. Charlotte had the impression that Carson Williamson could have been a pauper in the street and Sarah-Jane would have fallen for him in a heartbeat.

"Oh, good. We're here," said Thomas Brittler as the carriage drew to a halt in front of a large manor house. The gardens surrounding the vast dwelling were magnificent, even given the season. Neatly manicured hedges, leaves swaying in the cool evening breeze, lined a stone walkway. The house it led to was ablaze with lights, and Charlotte caught the sound of string music echoing out over the lawn. It was a captivating atmosphere, and she followed her sisters from the carriage, thinking that perhaps the party would not be a complete waste of time after all.

The house belonged to a man called Berkley Drexel. A man whom her father heartily disliked. He was an oil baron with, she had come to understand, considerable in-genuity in swindling others out of their money. Charlotte had never met him, of course, but she had listened to her father rage against him at the dinner table enough times to know that, had it not been for her mother's insistence, they would not be attending this gathering at all.

"Think of the people that will be in attendance," she had pleaded. "Think how it will look if we do not make an appearance. Everyone shall assume that you do not approve of Mr. Drexel. That you think he is beneath you."

"They would be right," Thomas had huffed, his great mustache blowing hither and thither in his agitation. "That man is a thief. His company is built on the backs of his unwilling and unknowing investors. He hasn't a cent to his own name."

You would never know it, thought Charlotte as she mounted the front steps of the manor. The foyer was decorated with marble and gilded gold. It was a rather ostentatious display. Her family had wealth, thanks to her father's sound investments and intelligent business decisions. His steel mills were flourishing, but their home did not display such a dramatic exhibition of their means. She could tell that the Drexel estate was designed to inspire envy in those less fortunate, and the thought made a hard lump rise in her throat. Whoever this Mr. Drexel was, he was bound to be a pretentious snot.

As they entered the lavish ballroom, Charlotte caught sight of a black-jacketed band in the corner. She hummed quietly under her breath along with the familiar notes of the 1812 Overture that emanated from their beautiful instruments. How she loved music.

A few onlookers milled around a crowded dance floor in the center of the room. Ornate gold and crystal chandeliers decorated the ceiling.

"Look," hissed Sarah in her ear as they made their way around the room, "He's here." She was indicating the tall, black-haired gentleman in the corner that was eyeing their party with every appearance of delight on his face.

"You knew he would be," said Charlotte, a crooked grin sliding over her lips as she took note of the excitement in her sister's voice. She didn't think Sarah heard her though as she strode forward to greet her suitor with their father by her side. Thomas Brittler made no secret of his approval for Sarah's beau. He received Carson enthusiastically, clasping his proffered hand in both of his own.

"Mr. Williamson. A pleasure to see you again."

Charlotte let her eyes wander over the crowd while they exchanged pleasantries. Her eyes fell on a young man that was sitting apart from the rest against the far wall. His eyes were closed and, for a moment, Charlotte thought he was asleep, but then she realized that he was listening to the music. He was on the shorter side, with a beard to rival her father's. Charlotte could tell that when he stood, he would only be an inch or two taller than her five feet and six inches. He was olive-skinned and gave an impression of great warmth, but he looked drawn, weary even. His broad, muscled shoulders were slumped. She cocked her head to the side, wondering if someone should attend to him, as he obviously wasn't well. Then his eyes opened, and they pierced her where she stood. They were the coldest shade of blue she had ever seen, almost colorless. His gaze stole the breath from her lungs, and she felt an eruption of sorts take place in her stomach.

The young man looked away from her to take a sip of his drink and Charlotte could breathe again. Her corset was feeling uncomfortably tight once more. She lifted her fan and spread the lace wide as a dull flush crept into her cheeks. She couldn't take her eyes from him. Who was he? She'd never seen him before.

Noelle nudged her gently with her elbow. "What are you staring at?" she asked. Her voice was low so as to not draw the attention of the others.

"Nothing," snapped Charlotte, recovering her senses. She turned her mind back to the conversation taking place before her, but she could feel the man's presence like a cold breath on the back of her neck.

They moved on after Sarah had promised a dance to Carson and the sisters made their way to a set of vacant seats against the far wall. Charlotte, embarrassed by her reaction to the blue-eyed stranger, did not look around for him again. Although, strangely, she sensed he was trying to catch her eye.

The music drifted over her and the evening made its own slow progress toward the dawn. Two hours later found Charlotte quite at her ease. She was conversing with an old acquaintance about the lessons she had been taking on the pianoforte when a shout of anger drew her attention across the room. She spotted the source of the disturbance at once and recognized the speaker with a jolt.

"I certainly do not take kindly to the idea you are suggesting, sir, and I would thank you to check your facts before leveling such accusatory contention in my family's direction." Blue-eyes turned from his adversary in a huff and straightened his waistcoat with a flourish. Then his gaze found Charlotte's once more. To her absolute shock, he made a beeline straight for her.

Charlotte could do nothing but watch him as he crossed the room to take hold of her gloved fingers and bow over her hand.

"Miss Brittler, might you favor me with this dance?"

After his none-too-quiet disagreement, every eye was upon them. Charlotte looked around for her mother or her father, wondering what on earth she should do. She was not acquainted with this man. They had never been introduced, and yet he spoke to her in the most familiar of tones, as though this dance he was asking for was a long-standing arrangement between the pair of them.

She hesitated for as long as she could whilst saving him from further embarrassment. "Yes, Mister-?" she prompted, rising to her feet as a soft violin began to play just behind her.

"Drexel, Miss. Logan Drexel."

Charlotte felt her eyes go wide as he led her onto the floor. She swallowed uncomfortably as Logan Drexel's arm encircled her waist and he pulled her into a flawless waltz. She blinked rapidly as those icy blue eyes found her, suddenly feeling like a mouse caught in the eyes of a snake.

"Have we-?"

"We have not been acquainted, miss. No. But I must admit, you caught my eye the moment you entered my father's home."

She felt her face color at his complement and she narrowed her gaze at him. "Is that so?" she asked suspiciously.

"It is," he said. He lowered his voice conspiratorially so that his warm breath brushed her ear and his lips quirked up delightfully in the corner. "I've an eye for beautiful things, you see."

"And an ear," said Charlotte. His hand was cold on her back. She could feel his touch through her many layers, and she felt gooseflesh rise up her arms. "I've noticed you seem to have a fondness for music."

He nodded as they spun in time with the fluid pace of the Gran Duo. "As I said," he responded. "Beautiful things."

Charlotte was unaccustomed to the attention Logan Drexel seemed to command. As he led her back to her seat against the wall, he bent low over her hand and, in full view of the entire room, he pressed his cool lips to her skin. An illicit thrill sped up her spine as he rose and the ice in his gaze pierced her. He smiled a very knowing smile, his thin lips pulled taut over his white teeth.

"Until we meet again, Miss Brittler," he said, still quietly, as though his words were for her ears alone. Then he was gone. He strode purposefully around the room and vanished through a door that led to the terrace.

The air seemed to clear. She could think again. One hundred pairs of eyes were fixed upon her. They took in her flushed face and her sheepish grin with wicked delight. Charlotte made an effort to compose herself as Noelle darted to her side.

"Who was that man?" she hissed into Charlotte's ear.

"Don't make a scene," Charlotte reprimanded, slapping her sister lightly with her fan.

"But who was he?" insisted Noelle. "I've never seen him before."

"That," said Charlotte as her insides calmed and embarrassment loosened its grip on her throat, "was the son of Berkley Drexel."

"He isn't."

"Yes, he is. His name is Logan."

"He would have to be handsome," Noelle said with a scowl.

"Of course," sighed Charlotte. She looked out over the dance floor, and she caught sight of Sarah dancing happily with her beau. "Did father see him dance with me?" she asked Noelle after a moment.

"No, he was in the library."

"Thank heavens for that." She didn't want another telling off about the Drexel family. She didn't need to hear it. She could have told any person who asked that Logan Drexel was not to be trusted. The way he had taken hold of her, though... As if he owned her. She felt an echo of the touch of his lips on the back of her hand and hastily scrubbed at it, fighting off the powerful sense of attraction that had filtered into her at his touch.

"I think it's all absolutely ridiculous," said Noelle. She was looking around the ballroom with interest. "The Drexel's are clearly flourishing. It's obvious they are of means. What on Earth could have turned Father so rigidly against them?"

"A bad business dealing can easily sour a man's impression of another," suggested Charlotte with a shrug.

Logan entered the room once more. His back was straight as he made his way through the crowd, stopping to chat amicably with a set of twin girls that looked to be around Noelle's age. Their names were Angela and Abigail Darling. Their father owned a large chain of apothecaries.

Charlotte couldn't help but watch Logan, and she was surprised by the sudden pang of jealousy that overtook her as she watched him bend to kiss each of the girls' hands in farewell. Her cheeks flushed. This then, was how he treated all the available women he met. She had been a fool to think she was a special case.

He moved like a cat, sliding through spaces that looked much too small for him. Stopping to exchange with various acquaintances for only moments at a time. As he made to leave the entrance hall, his attention was caught by a tall brunette. She smiled invitingly at Logan, and Charlotte again felt that sudden wave of jealousy. Of ownership. It took her a moment to realize what this feeling was. Competition.

She was a quietly combative woman. And for some reason, after having reacted so strongly to her first impression of Logan, her mind had staked a claim. She tried to drown the feeling as she took a healthy swallow of the punch Noelle had just handed her, but the sensation only grew.

She wasn't listening to her sister prattle; she wasn't aware of her surroundings. She could only watch as the brunette brushed her fingers along Logan's jacketed shoulder, and feel her blood began to boil.

She stood up.

"Where are you going?" asked Noelle with a whine, struggling to her feet as well. Charlotte didn't answer her.

She tossed a dangling strand of red hair back from her face and moved purposefully towards Logan Drexel.

The brunette noticed her coming. She eyed Charlotte with a look of contempt over Mister Drexel's shoulder as she drew nearer. When he turned, he did not look surprised to see Charlotte standing behind him. In fact, Charlotte noticed as she took a deep breath and opened her mouth to speak, the look in his eye was one of vague satisfaction. He took a sip of his drink, looking heartily amused.

"Miss Brittler," he said in warm greeting. "Won't you join us?" His eyes danced playfully and Charlotte hesitated, flummoxed. What had she intended to say to him?

Those cold blue eyes were boring into her.

Charlotte Brittler was not shy. She was generally very comfortable in her skin. Why, then, was this man tying her up in knots? After one dance, no less!

She opened her mouth once more, but no sound came out. The tall brunette smiled coyly.

"I think your new friend has forgotten her voice on the other side of the room," she said with a laugh.

Something snapped into place at these words. "On the contrary," smiled Charlotte, "I was merely caught off guard by the rather boisterous exhibition on the front of your dress, Miss Carlisle."

The brunette flushed at the barb and glanced down at the large and glittery brooch pinned just below her—rather low—neckline. "Yes. Lovely, isn't it?" she said, recovering herself. "It's been in my family for generations. Thank you for noticing it."

"Generations," responded Charlotte with another wry grin. "Of course. Although, I doubt your grandmother wore it quite so boldly upon her bosom. I would hope that, as your matron, your grandmother would display a more distinct sense of tact."

Miss Carlisle's already blushing cheeks deepened to crimson and she hastily excused herself. Charlotte stepped into her place, drawing Logan Drexel's full attention onto herself.

He looked pleased with her boldness. "I must say," he said, glancing towards Miss Carlisle's—now retreating—back. "I've never been able to understand why the young ladies insist on jewelry that will most assuredly cause them back pain by the end of the evening." He slumped forward in jest, as though being pulled down by a great weight dangling from his shirtfront, and Charlotte chuckled appreciatively.

"They wish to draw the eyes," she said, indicating Miss Carlisle's newest endeavor. A young man by the name of Alec Langley, who couldn't seem to help himself from examining the brooch with interest.

Logan smiled. "And yet there are those who are beautiful enough that the eye is drawn of its own accord," he said.

Charlotte watched his eyes flicker over her form and she felt her own narrow dangerously. "Wandering eyes aren't a commonly appreciated quality in most men, Mister Drexel," she said through her teeth. Although she wasn't sure that she would stand by that statement. His wandering eyes were making her feel something like a goddess and she couldn't decide if she disliked the feeling or not.

"Of course," whispered Mister Drexel, inclining his head. "Could I entice you into another dance?"

Charlotte was deliberating, on the point of agreeing, when she caught sight of something that made her face pale. Her father. He was standing poker-straight in the ballroom entrance, his expression very sour indeed.

"You'll have to excuse me, Mister Drexel, but I'm afraid I have promised this dance to another," she said stoically.

With that, she spun around and made her way over to an old acquaintance.

His name was Carl Grimsby, a man who had long nursed a soft spot for her and her sisters. He was rather round-faced and had a tendency to sweat quite a lot, but he was friendly. She had no trouble eliciting a dance from him, and she fell quickly into the familiar steps, trying not to catch her father's eye. She giggled and laughed at Mr. Grimsby's least amusing comments, all the while feeling two sets of eyes on her back as she moved. The pair belonging to her father was wary, angry, and irascible. However, the second pair, those cold, icy blue eyes that raked her hemline and scanned her cheeks for a blush, those entirely captivating eyes... they looked hungry.

Her father set upon her like an angry wolf as soon as she had bid farewell to her dancing partner. "I noticed you were quite eager to distance yourself from your conversation with Mister Drexel," he said under his breath. His eyes smoldered, the only indicator of his fury. His smile was benign, and to any of the passers-by, he would have looked unperturbed.

Charlotte felt it was best to be honest. "I didn't think you would like me talking to him, Father."

Thomas Brittler relaxed visibly at these words. "You know the kind of man his father is," he muttered, nodding at old Mister Dillensby as he passed them on his way to the tables. "I have seen no proof that his son's ideals vary from his."

"Have you heard or seen anything to the contrary? Perhaps young Mister Drexel disagrees with his father's practices." Charlotte fiddled with the seam in her glove, not looking at her father. She was desperate not to convey her interest in the man.

Thomas Brittler's eyes hardened infinitesimally. "I don't want you marrying into that family."

"It was one dance, Father!" exclaimed Charlotte, her exasperation evident in her voice. "I haven't asked to marry the man!"

"You danced with him?"

Charlotte gulped, realizing her mistake as Thomas swelled with fury. "I didn't know his name at the time," she said quickly, laying her gloved hand on her father's forearm to ease his retaliation. "I only learned who he was after I had already agreed to the dance."

This time, her father caught her eye. His gaze was steady and his mustache bristled as he bared down upon her. "That boy is off limits," he barked.

Charlotte stood her ground. "You know nothing about him," she said stubbornly, raising her chin. Her father caught hold of her arm and Charlotte's eyes widened at the ferocity of his reaction.

"You'll obey me, Charlotte. He's trouble. He will do you nothing but harm." He gave her arm a little shake, as though hoping her good sense would return with the movement. "I can see your interest in your defense of his character, but I will not permit it. Remove the idea from your mind and have done with it."

He released her and stalked away. Smiling at all the other guests in attendance, he returned to the party. Charlotte's cheeks were crimson once more. As she straightened her skirts and beamed around the crowded dance floor, she felt tears prick her eyes.

CHAPTER TWO

———— ✦ ————

"HE CAN'T BE SERIOUS," said Samantha Brittler.

It was a week since the night of the Drexel's gathering. One long, dreadful week since Logan Drexel had caught her eye. Charlotte had been unable to think of anything else since those cold, blue eyes had pierced her. Never in her life had she suffered from such an all-consuming obsession.

"He certainly is," she responded to her mother. It was early morning. A dim, pink light was flooding into the carriage from the Eastern horizon as it trundled along the path towards the city.

Samantha Brittler was looking askance at her daughter, her thin brows pulling together in the middle. A thin woman, with her hair in a tight bun at the base of her neck, Charlotte's mother was never someone to trifle with. She had a very no-nonsense attitude towards courting illustrious matches for each of her four daughters, and Charlotte was no exception.

"The Drexel's are of good standing. Berkley Drexel has sound investments in many qualified business dealings. His son would certainly be a respectable match."

"Mother," said Charlotte for what felt like the hundredth time. "You know Father's opinion of the man. He would never allow me to marry—"

"Hmm..." said Samantha, pursing her lips.

They did not speak again until they arrived at the shops in the main square, on which point Samantha continued to gripe, seeming unable to help herself.

"I mean," she said, her voice low as they strolled up the aisles of a fabric depot. "There are so few eligible gentlemen," she stressed the word, "in town. It's a wonder he expects you to marry at all."

Charlotte glared at her mother's back as she moved away from her.

Their father wanted them to marry for love and happiness. Their mother wanted them to marry for wealth and means. "A stable, secure life for my girls," she would say, "that's what I want for them."

Between her parents' two opposing opinions on the matter, the Brittler girl's choices were very limited. When it all came down to it, though, her father had the final say in things. Samantha may wheedle and whine, but she would always give in. Up until this very moment, in fact, Charlotte had been very grateful for her father's intervention. Up until that very moment, she'd had absolutely no objections to asking for her father's assistance in the matter. Now, though, when his opinion was controversial to her own, she was—as was natural—beginning to accept that her mother may have possessed a valuable argument. Logan Drexel was not only enticing and handsome, but he was possessed of the means to care for her comfortably for the rest of her life.

Security. A handsome and wealthy husband on her arm? She had to admit, the idea was quite alluring. But... would she love him? Charlotte pursed her lips as she trailed her fingers over the corner of a bolt of smooth, red velvet. Love was something she required. She had grown up in a house where her mother and father had snuck kisses in front of the fireplace in the parlor and teased one another in small, playful ways. Despite their grievances, theirs had been a love match.

Samantha had been a young, childless widow when she married Thomas. It had been an advantageous marriage on both sides, but their meeting had been incidental. Their spark had been genuine.

Because of this, Samantha was under the impression that both love and wealth could be attained simultaneously, while Thomas felt that love was in the foremost of the qualities one should look for in a potential relationship. There had been little discrepancy on the matter for a good long time. That was, until Dianna had departed for the Wyoming territory in the fall.

Samantha wanted each of her daughters to marry for security. That was her goal. A happy, content life of prosperity and customary comforts, far above the reproach of society. In her defense, what mother would want anything different for her offspring?

Charlotte pretended to examine a scrap of lace, twirling it idly between her thumb and forefinger.

"That would be a very fitting color for your complexion."

Charlotte looked around, expecting to see her mother. She was met instead with a steady, ice-blue gaze that lifted the hairs on the back of her arms. She'd only seen eyes like that once before.

"Mrs. Felicity Drexel, my dear. We crossed paths at the quaint little gathering my husband and I hosted last week."

"Oh, yes! Of course." Charlotte felt her cheeks coloring up at once. She did indeed remember having been introduced to their hostess. It had been in passing, and Charlotte's attention had been so focused on Logan Drexel that she couldn't recall a word of her previous conversation with his mother.

Mrs. Drexel was now examining her critically. "Yes, I do think that color would suit you well," she said, taking the scrap of lace from Charlotte's hand and holding it up to the light. "Perhaps you should use it to trim your wedding gown."

Charlotte's blush deepened, but she straightened her shoulders at these words. There was no reason for Mrs. Drexel to know that her insides were suddenly dancing the polka. "I'm afraid the idea is far from my mind at the moment," she lied smoothly. "I've few passable prospects on the horizon."

"Really?" whispered Mrs. Drexel, with a smirk that was not unlike her son's. "I think you might find that changing very soon."

And on that enigmatic note, she winked at Charlotte and strolled away up the aisle.

Charlotte watched her go, feeling elated. Her imagination was conjuring up image after image. Fantasies that she hadn't given a passing thought to since she was a little girl. Dreams of a white dress, of a house large enough to require a handful of servants. Of a beaming husband, beside whom she would sit as their children played on the parlor floor. She sighed and looked down at the lace in her hand. It felt coarse between her fingers, but she could just picture it lining a long veil and trailing down the bodice of her wedding gown.

She looked up again as her mother approached her, a broad grin plastered all over her face.

"I've just met Mrs. Drexel coming up the other side of the store," she squeaked, taking hold of Charlotte's wrist. "She's invited us to lunch at their home on Saturday next."

Charlotte felt her eyes go wide for a moment, and then she smiled. Without hesitation, she lifted the lace from the shelf and carried it over to the counter. She could feel Mrs. Drexel's eyes on her back as she ordered the entire bolt.

❧

"Father's not going to like this," hissed Charlotte, leaning across the carriage to pluck a stray thread from her mother's sleeve.

Samantha Brittler frowned at her daughter. They were once again ensconced in the family carriage as it made its ungainly way towards their destination. "What your father doesn't know won't do him any harm at all," she muttered. She waved a dismissive hand in irritation. "We're just having lunch with the woman, not her son. There is no danger of— Oh, dear." She broke off as they rounded a bend, and the Drexel's large manor house circled into their limited view.

Several well-dressed gentlemen were cantering around the far-flung—and immaculately kept— front lawns on horseback. They were each in possession of a heavy-looking mallet, with which they appeared to be striking at a wooden ball in the grass. "What are they doing?" asked Samantha Brittler, aghast.

Charlotte bent forward, the better to see the interesting display taking place before them. "It's polo," she laughed after a moment, sitting back in her seat as the carriage came to a jolting halt a short distance from the front door.

Her mother shot her a disgusted look. "I can see that it's polo," she said as the footman opened the side door with a yank. "I was merely inquiring as to why they might choose to partake in such an un-American pastime upon the Drexel's front lawn."

Charlotte rolled her eyes at her mother's back. Then she gathered her skirts and heaved herself from the carriage door. It was quite rich to hear her mother talk of anything being un-American when she herself was originally from England.

As they made their way up the wide front steps, Charlotte tried not to glance around at the joyous shouts of sport echoing over the emerald green lawns. She was half-way up before the sound of her own name made her turn. She knew who had spoken without looking, but that did not make the sight of Logan Drexel's blue eyes any less shocking on her senses. She swallowed and greeted him with a confident smile and the nod of her head.

"Mr. Drexel," she said in greeting, feeling warmth seep into her outer extremities as his cold eyes glued her feet to the stone beneath them. "A pleasure to see you again."

"The pleasure is all mine," he said. He moved up the steps slowly, his eyes fixed on hers. "My mother mentioned that you would be stopping by today. I beg you to excuse the uproar. The Westchester Polo Club asked to meet here on the first Saturday of each month, and as I am a senior member, I am generally obliged to accommodate their wishes." He inclined his head subserviently and somehow managed to look just that as his eyes found hers once more. "You'll forgive my forwardness," he said. "But if you don't mind my saying so, you look positively ravishing this afternoon."

Charlotte stared at him. She couldn't put her finger on it. There was something odd in his expression. As though he was playing a part. She dismissed this thought as she accepted the compliment with thanks and spun around to introduce her mother, who was waiting for her on the top step.

Samantha preened as Logan climbed the remaining stairs and planted a kiss on the back of her hand. "It is very clear to me that Charlotte has inherited her mother's beauty," he said, straightening.

Charlotte grinned. Her mother was very susceptible to flattery.

Sure enough, Samantha began fanning herself vigorously as the young Mr. Drexel excused himself to rejoin his teammates.

"Oh my," she sighed, watching him walk away with a girlish flush blooming on her face. Then she glanced at her daughter. "He's a catch, that one," she said. "My dear, if you do not marry him, I shall."

Charlotte snorted with laughter as a liveried butler admitted them into the cavernous foyer of the Drexel house.

Lunch with Mrs. Drexel was a stuffy affair. Charlotte found her mind wandering aimlessly as the woman droned on and on about this thing or that. There was many 'Did you hears' as well as a few 'well, I nevers' from both her mother and Logan's.

Charlotte's attention was not caught until Mrs. Drexel's bright blue gaze fell onto her and she straightened herself up in the most business-like manner. It looked as though she were readying herself to make a proclamation on behalf of the King.

"I'm sure it has not escaped your notice," she began, dabbing at the edges of her— rather wide— mouth with the corner of a napkin. "That my son has developed an interest in your company."

Samantha Brittler choked on the minuscule bite of sandwich she had just taken. She looked around at Mrs. Drexel with her eyes watering and took a hasty sip of water. Charlotte sat back in her chair. For a moment, the only sounds that permeated the air were the masculine shouts of laughter echoing from the front lawn.

"I am also aware," continued Mrs. Drexel, "that your father would be disinclined to allow such a courtship to blossom within his home. I would, therefore, like to invite you to visit the Drexel house regularly in favor of furthering my son's interest in you."

Charlotte set down the glass of water she had been about to take a sip of. It landed on the table a bit harder than she meant it to and she saw her mother wince.

"Why?" Charlotte saw Samantha wince again at the harsh note in her voice.

"Why?" repeated Mrs. Drexel, an incredulous smile spreading over her face. "I intend to ensure my son's happiness, Miss Brittler. That is why."

Charlotte felt a smile creep up her face as her eyes darted over Mrs. Drexel's. Was she being serious? Of course, a woman pressing her company upon a man in his home would be a bit of a departure from tradition. It was generally the other way around. But...that would also mean defying her father.

She glanced at her mother, whose brows had slid up into her hairline. She took a fraction of a second to ponder her conscience and then opened her mouth.

"Your offer is gracious," she said. Charlotte swallowed the hard lump that had risen into her throat. "But I am afraid that I must-"

"She must have some time to consider the matter," Samantha interrupted smoothly. "And it is not for lack of interest in your son, let me assure you." She smiled warmly and patted their hostess on the hand. "It is out of respect for her father's wishes that my daughter hesitates."

Mrs. Drexel looked for a moment as though she were trying to swallow a large chestnut whole, but then she too smiled. Charlotte couldn't help but notice that her smile didn't quite meet her eyes.

"Of course. We wouldn't want to do anything that might cause a rift between a father and his daughter," she said coolly. "But be advised. Logan has—shall we say—a marginal amount of patience. You may soon find him under your roof whether you like it or not."

Charlotte raised an eyebrow in mock challenge. "I suppose we should arm ourselves to the hilt, Mother," she said.

Samantha Brittler laughed and the tension broke.

Charlotte paced around her room, glancing towards the open doorway every few minutes or so. The conversation taking place between her parents downstairs had risen in volume as her father's temper heated. She could just make out the sound of his thunderous voice echoing up the stairs.

"...Did you even give it a thought, Samantha? What possessed you...?"

Her mother's reply was so quiet that—strain her ears though she might–Charlotte couldn't make it out. A few seconds later, however, her father's deep baritone made such efforts quite unnecessary.

"You know! I've told you before what kind of man that boy's father is. Would you really wish to press that kind of relationship on our daughter?"

"He seemed like a decent young man to me. Really, Thomas. You can't hold on to..."

"Hold on to!? Hold on to?! His father robbed us blind, Samantha. Stole Dianna's dowry right out from under our noses!"

"You've never had any proof…"

"Proof?!" Thomas Brittler's outrage seemed to render him temporarily speechless. Charlotte had seen this point in his rages before. Her father had finally reached the brink of frustration that defied explanation. "That is enough of this. I won't have Charlotte anywhere near the Drexel boy. That is my final word. If she even breathes near him, I'll disown her."

Charlotte gasped and stumbled away from the door. Disown her? Surely he didn't mean it. She felt her knees trembling and reached blindly for the edge of her mattress. That was that. There would be no more question to the matter. There should never have been a question to it in the first place, whispered an unbidden voice in the back of her mind.

She heard the truth in these words. Despite her recent resentment of the restrictions her father had placed on her, she understood. She respected his decision. And now she knew there was an ironclad reason behind her father's opinions.

Berkley Drexel had stolen Dianna's dowry? How? How could he have possibly gotten away with such a crime? Despite her confusion, facts began to crash into place inside her mind.

Her eldest sister had been beautiful. She had been hot-tempered, yes, and perhaps a bit difficult to please, but essentially kind-hearted. This was the reason she remained unmarried for so long. Why hadn't her father told his daughters what had happened? Dianna was twelve years her senior. She had been born a good long while before any of the other Brittler sisters. By every common rule in the book, she ought to have been married long before them. Had she known of the catastrophe? Would it have mattered? She doubted it. Dianna had never been content, she reminded herself. She would have gone in search of an adventure one way or another. A bizarre wave of comfort overtook Charlotte. It was so forceful, that for a moment she couldn't breathe. The knowledge that this horrible incident had had little to no effect on Dianna's future was a blessing. She sent up a silent prayer of thanks and begged for the strength she would need to conquer the strange, otherworldly temptation that was Logan Drexel.

Chapter Three

Logan cleared his throat as he entered his father's study. It was a large room, sumptuously decorated, with high ceilings and an elaborate crystal chandelier dangling from the center-most beam. His parents had spared no expense when they built the shining palace of a home on the outer edges of Manhattan. A large bay window encompassed most of the wall on his right, providing startling views of the harbor below. The glorious picture was wasted, however. Logan didn't even glance at the picturesque surroundings outside the glass.

He made his way toward the desk situated against the opposite wall and the man sitting behind it. Berkley Drexel didn't glance up as his son moved toward him around the many over-stuffed poufs and high-backed armchairs dotting the room.

"You're late," he said, by way of a greeting. Logan gritted his teeth and did not respond. He clasped his hands behind his back and waited.

His father finished scribbling a note to his haggard solicitor and took his time folding it in thirds before he finally looked up. "I'd like an update on the situation with the Brittler girl."

Logan frowned. He had expected this. "I've very little to report," he said stiffly.

His father's bushy eyebrows lifted in mock surprise. "Really? Is she proving difficult to sway?"

Logan glared at him. "I've had limited opportunities to communicate with her since Mother asked her to luncheon last weekend."

Berkley Drexel slammed his fist on the table in fury. "Then make an opportunity," he barked, leaping to his feet.

Logan watched him as he hobbled around the desk. His father was a few inches shorter than him, but his silhouette was still impressive. The expensive black wig he usually wore was a little lopsided this morning, as though he had squashed it onto his head in a hurry when he'd heard Logan coming down the stairs.

"Do I need to remind you how important it is for you to secure a marriage with that girl?" His father came right up to him and poked him in the chest. Logan's frown deepened, and he exhaled slowly, trying to reign in his temper. "Funds are dwindling, Logan! And Thomas Brittler is secure. Once you've attached yourself to his daughter, you'll inherit the generous dowry he has, no doubt, set aside for her. And after that is gone, we'll be able to milk him for more. Thomas Brittler," he spat the name, "wouldn't ever refuse anything to his darling, little debutante daughters."

Logan took a step back from his father and eyed the gray hairs poking out from beneath his wig. "I understand the importance of the situation," he said with a sour note in his voice. "But the circumstances cannot be helped. Thomas won't let me anywhere near her. He suspects you had something to do with the breach in his bank's security all those years ago."

"How can he possibly suspect me?" An evil grin slid onto Berkley Drexel's face. "The money was rightfully mine!"

Logan sighed and glanced out the bay window. A seagull flew past it, screeching its horrible song to the myriad of boats below. He was well accustomed to his father's habit of self-justification. His various acts of embezzlement were, in his opinion, money he was entitled to in the first place.

Logan didn't have a reason to disagree with him, although he was starting to think that he should. He'd been raised under the same guise as every other person in Manhattan. That his father, Berkley Drexel, had obtained his wealth through smart investments and intelligent business dealings. As he had grown from a child into a man, his father had begun to request things from him.

They seemed like insignificant acts at first. The first had come into play when Logan had been fifteen. His friend, Johnathan Scott, had been the son of his father's foremost competitor in the oil industry.

"All I need," Berkley Drexel had said, his large knuckles resting on Logan's thin shoulder, "is a story. Something that suggests Avery Scott's practices are not up to par."

And so, Logan had spied. He'd stolen letters and listened at keyholes until there finally came a day when he was no longer welcomed at the Scott's townhouse. Avery Scott's business inadvertently fell into shambles. His father had gotten what he wanted, Logan was relieved.

And then when he was seventeen, his task had been to court the goddaughter of an illustrious businessman. His father had never given him a reason but had demanded that the assignment be carried out. He had been nearly engaged to the poor girl when Berkley had launched his newest proposal to her godfather. Excited about the union of their families, the man had invested several thousand dollars into Berkley's scheme. However, Berkley's promises never came to fruition, and he soon gave Logan permission to end the courtship.

They had continued in this vein for many years, Logan never finding any reason to doubt his father's motives. He, surely, acted with only the welfare of his family in mind. But as Logan grew into manhood, he began to suspect the older man of an ulterior ambition.

"This is the last time," he said through his teeth, still not looking at his father. "I will carry you no further in these endeavors. When this is over, that's the end."

Berkley's expression hardened as he gazed at his only son. He straightened the hem of his impeccably cut suit. "Have you no pity," he asked, a note of woe in his voice.

Had Logan been looking at his father, he would have seen the small transformation that took place on his features. His brows softened; the muscles relaxed perceptibly. His eyes lost their steely glint. It was a show. A carefully orchestrated display of submission and suffering.

When Logan turned back to his father, the man seemed to have shrunken. "We need you," Berkley bleated helplessly. "Your mother and I cannot manage on our own."

Logan's expression was unmoved. He stared coldly down the tip of his long nose at his father and raised a superior brow.

"What kind of man relies on the deception of others to fuel his own happiness?" he said.

His father reeled back from him as though Logan had struck him a physical blow.

"These... deceptions—as you call them— have paid for your way of living time and time again. The meager funds I have rightly earned from my companions in the business industry are insignificant to the men that would claim them. These people have coffers overflowing with their stumbled upon wealth." Berkley shrugged. "I have merely exacted a small fee which the law does not deem fit to entitle me to."

Logan rolled his eyes. He'd heard the same words time and time again. His father was under the impression that you could rework the same sentence one million times over and still achieve the desired effect each time. The unfortunate thing was, this tactic often worked. Just not on Logan. Not anymore.

"The law does not entitle you to it for a reason, Father," Logan whispered. He ignored the thick anger that clouded Berkley Drexel's features and slid across the room to stare down at the harbor. "I will be departing Manhattan in two months' time."

He heard his father began to sputter but spoke over him.

"I will be traveling west to cultivate dealings with Stephen Harkness about a possible merger with Standard Oil."

This was the first mention he had made of his plans. Berkley Drexel's stammering ceased abruptly. Logan had the impression that his father had lost the ability to draw breath.

"If the merger is successful, you will affix me as your partner in the running of Drexel Industries. I will control all financial increase and decrease in what remains of the business. After a short period, you will announce me as your successor."

Berkley coughed. Speech would invariably return to him, and soon. Logan glanced over his shoulder. A well-worn vein throbbed in his father's temple as his faced purpled with the extent of his outrage.

"Wha-what makes you think you have the authority to make demands such as these? You have no power over me. You are my heir. You will do as I say. Your mistaken impression of…"

"You will do as I have asked," interrupted Logan. He turned to face his father. The gray light of the skies beyond the window glazed the room, sucking all color from the crimson draperies and illuminating the dust that sat thick on every surface. The room was filthy, despite its splendor. They'd had to reduce their household staff after his father's most recent loss at the gambling tables.

"I won't bow to you, Logan," muttered his father, swelling with indignation. "I-"

"You have proved time and time again that you are incapable of making any decisions that do not directly benefit your selfish aspirations. You do not do for the good of the company or for your family. Your plans and various means of retaining your social status and wealth endanger everything my grandfather worked for." He swallowed and stared up to the place above the mantle where his grandfather's baleful portrait hung.

"My conscience can no longer permit me to sit by and watch the destabilization of our company and our home," he said with a finality bordering on indifference. "If you refuse, I will contact the authorities and inform them of your—less than savory—business dealings. I would rather go down with you now than to allow us to continue along the path that will lead to a more brutal end."

Berkley opened his mouth and then closed it. He opened it again, looking something like a goldfish relieved of its bowl. "But you'll need funds!" he gasped finally. "You'll need something with which to tempt Harkness. He'll not be interested without the promise of gain."

Logan sighed and his shoulders slumped. He felt the fight and anger leave him for a moment, and he leaned back onto the window frame. The face of the Brittler girl flashed before his eyes. He saw the brilliant red of her hair and the fascinated distaste with which she seemed to view him.

"This shall be the last time," he breathed. "A marriage of convenience is not, after all, illegal."

Chapter Four

It was impressive and bewildering. Such a dramatic sensation of grief had overtaken Charlotte that she found the oppression of her own emotions to be an unwieldy burden upon her physique. It was with desperation that she exited the Brittler house and made her way down the short drive to the through road. She needed air.

Dressed to ward off the chill of the coming winter, she inhaled deeply as she turned left towards town.

Charlotte had spent the day in the company of her sisters, Noelle and Sarah-Jane. Neither of which was disposed to be very sympathetic to her plight.

"You should never have danced with him," griped Noelle. She had her legs crossed on the velvety pouf in front of her armchair and she had fixed Charlotte with a most Dianna-ish look as she said this. "He's put you under some sort of devilish spell."

"Don't talk nonsense," snapped Sarah-Jane. She had her latest embroidery project in her lap and did not look up until Charlotte sank down onto the settee beside her.

"Noelle's right," Charlotte whispered. Her hands felt clammy. "I'm not even sure what to say. I don't even like the man."

"Then it's settled," said Sarah matter-of-factly. She held her hoop up to the light of the window to make out the faint pattern on the white fabric. "If you never even cared for Logan Drexel, why should it matter that you are no longer permitted to be in his company."

"That's just it," sighed Charlotte, moving restlessly over to the library window, "I don't know." She bit her lip and glanced down at Noelle, who was wearing a look of smug disapproval.

"It's because he's off limits. That's why you want him."

"That's absolutely untrue," Charlotte protested. "I didn't know who he was the first time I saw him, did I?"

"Maybe not," growled Noelle, crossing her arms over her chest, "but you certainly made no effort to avoid his attentions once you did know."

Charlotte remembered the unusual spike of jealousy that had shot through her when she had seen the beautiful Miss Carlisle sinking her claws into Logan, and her heart leaped into her throat. What was wrong with her? Why should it have mattered? She'd had but one dance with the man. One.

One dance that had stolen her breath. One dance that had demanded her attention— all of it— be focused on the man whose icy gaze could send shivers down her spine. She felt a chill creep down her back at the memory.

"It will do you no good to moan about it," said Sarah-Jane, ever the practical one. She straightened her embroidery cloth and looked up. "You can't have him."

"It wouldn't have stopped Di," whispered Noelle.

Charlotte darted a glance at her younger sister. Noelle smiled naughtily.

"I'm nothing like Dianna," Charlotte retorted. She turned on her heel and stomped out of the room, her heart thundering in her ears.

Her thoughts were a tangled mess as she made her way along the high street. The day was bitterly cold and the wind bit at her cheeks. Before long, they had turned red and numb, but Charlotte kept walking. It felt good to do something. To take some sort of action, even if that action would do nothing to assuage the small, burning ache that had developed in the pit of her stomach.

She was still reeling from the conversation she had overheard between her mother and father.

"I'll disown her."

That's what her father had said. Disown her? She had been terrified at first and offended that her father cared so little for her that he would be able to ostracize her without a second thought. It had taken several painful hours for her to come to the conclusion that that was not the case. It was out of fear for her safety that he had spoken. He'd been determined to stress his point, to strike it home. Her interest—if it could even be called that— with Logan Drexel had driven her father to the point of terror. And her mother's enthusiasm for the idea had caused him to speak harshly to deter her.

She pictured the look on his face the night of the Drexel's gathering. When her father had seen with whom she was speaking, Thomas Brittler's expression had gone through a myriad of emotions. Shock, terror, then fury. All in the space of about five seconds. She knew, deep down, how his desire to keep her safe should have affected her. What her reaction should have been. But instead of losing interest in Logan immediately, she had pursued another "chance" meeting with him.

Well, that was the end. It didn't matter if young Mr. Drexel had begun cropping up in her dreams in ways that made her blush when she woke. It didn't matter that her eyes searched crowds for him of their own accord. None of it mattered. He was not an option. She would have to do her best to forget all abou-.

She had walked into something very warm and very solid and she squealed with alarm as she nearly toppled over backward into the street.

"Miss Brittler?" said a most familiar voice, sounding pleasurably flustered. A gloved hand caught hold of her upper arm and steadied her. Surely, she hadn't just walked into... she looked up and met Logan Drexel's icy blue gaze. He was as flushed as she was with the cold of the late afternoon. His skin—looking much like strong tea and cream—was pink in places. He looked deliciously refresh-ing.

Her heart gave an unpleasant throb, and she realized that she was staring. Her breath caught in her throat. He was looking at her, his smile grew a little puzzled as her fear began to sink in, and Charlotte knew it must be showing on her face. She glanced around. The street was empty. Very few people seemed prepared to brave the freezing temperatures in town today.

"Logan," she hadn't meant to whisper his name.

His eyebrows flew up and she felt his grip tighten on her forearm. All at once, realization crashed down on her. If anyone should see her. Anyone. What if they mentioned it to her father? Her eyes darted around the empty square once more, and without warning, she seized Mr. Drexel's lapel and tugged him out of sight, down a small alleyway between two townhouses.

Logan's mouth popped open in surprise and his eyes went wide.

"What are you—?"

"Shhh," she whispered, without really knowing why she was shushing him. There was no one around to hear them. She peeked around the corner and then looked back at her quarry.

Logan appeared to be hiding a smile. He was biting his lips as though determined his amusement would not show on his face.

"May I ask why we are hiding from non-existent eyes?"

Charlotte looked at him seriously and began to speak. "Your mother has made your interest in me known," she said. Her voice was quiet, and he had to incline his ear to hear her. "I must tell you-" she halted. The sounds of an approaching cart could be heard over the near silent rhythm of their breathing. Charlotte shrank back into the shadows behind Logan as the jingling and clopping sounds came nearer and nearer, finally passing their little alcove and making its way further down the street.

Logan was still eyeing her with every appearance of smug amusement.

"I must tell you that your attentions will not be welcome."

"Not welcome?" chuckled Logan disbelievingly. He was looking down at her, and that penetrating light blue gaze seemed to see into her very soul.

Charlotte felt warmth seep into her bones and she realized that he had yet to release her. They were standing very close together in the tight space. She took a hasty step back. Logan's hand came free of her upper arm, leaving her feeling bereft.

She crossed her own arms in front of her chest and rubbed them slowly, shivering. She hadn't been aware of how cold she was until this moment. Until Logan Drexel was standing so close to her that she could feel warmth emanating from him in waves. He smelled masculine. A hint of hickory smoke and some vague spice that she couldn't put her finger on. She found she was breathing very deeply, despite her fear.

"Not welcome," she repeated firmly, as much to herself as to Logan. Charlotte looked up. He was so close to her.

"You offend me, Miss," he whispered, still smiling. "I was under the impression that you rather fancied me." He raised his hand casually and ran a finger down her cheek.

Charlotte felt fire erupt in the wake of his touch. The sensation startled her, for it was accompanied by the most confounding lurch of anger. She slapped his hand away. "I am sorry to inform you that you've been very misled, and I'd thank you for keeping your hands to yourself in future."

Her hand stung where it had struck his. The cold had filtered into her fingers and turned them numb. Judging by Logan's flinch, the sting of the blow had caught him off guard as well. He shook his hand out, now looking irritated.

But then he smiled. It was like watching a mask slide over his face. A gently placating grin replaced his look of irritation, and Charlotte's eyes narrowed. Something was off. He was trying too hard.

She took another step away from him as he spoke. "Come now, Miss Brittler," he said. He held out a slim hand to her. "Why don't we discuss this somewhere warmer?" He looked so inviting, and she was so very cold.

Charlotte shook her head violently from side to side. "My father does not think we would make an acceptable match. I wish to discourage you from any further advances."

"And so, your father rules your opinions?" Logan asked. He seemed to be trying and failing to look as if this was a throw-away question, but something in his expression told her that his words held particular meaning to him. She straightened her back.

"I am my own woman."

"...I see..." said Logan slowly. It could not have been clearer that he did not believe a single word of that statement. Charlotte bristled, but Logan held up his hand. "I understand that it is easier for some women to simply abide by the whim and opinions of others..."

The same fury that had ignited within her when his finger had casually slid over her cheek lanced through her once more at his words. Is that what he thought she was doing? Simply collapsing beneath the pressure of her father's demands? Did he think that she was so fragile, so dependent on the will of others, that she would not stand her ground when her opinions differed from theirs? She felt her nails biting into her palms.

Without warning, she lifted her heeled boot and brought it smashing down onto Logan's toes.

He yelped and his rambling speech about the ease of a woman's lot in life was cut short. Charlotte glared at him as he hopped before her on one foot.

"Forgive me," she spat. "But your powers of observation are sorely lacking. Your misguided interpretations of my actions have only reaffirmed my first impression of your character, and I regret to say that it was not a pleasant one. Good day."

Without offering Logan a curtsy or even a nod of her head, she slid out of the alley and stormed away down the street.

Was there ever a man so arrogant as Logan Drexel? Charlotte's chest heaved with indignation as she stalked across the frozen ground. The nerve of him! He spoke to her as though she was nothing more than a child. How had she ever found him attractive?

It seemed impossible that she had awoken that morning feeling distraught by her father's edict. After the conversation she had just had with the man, how could she blame him? Logan Drexel evidently had no regard for anyone other than himself.

"Miss Brittler! Miss Brittler, please wait!"

He was coming after her. Really. Had he no shame?

She spun on the spot, her fury climbing still higher. "I cannot imagine a way that I could have made myself and my feelings more clear-" but she halted as she saw the man that faced her.

Mr. Grimsby appeared quite heartbroken at her words. He'd covered his prematurely balding head with a black bowler, and his second chin was carefully concealed in the thick scarf he had wrapped around his neck.

"Oh!" exclaimed Charlotte, startled. She tilted sideways to peer behind Mr. Grimsby's squat bulk but saw no sign of Logan Drexel anywhere. Her eyes scanned the buildings on either side of them, fixating on the spaces between the houses. Nothing.

Mr. Grimsby was looking troubled. "If my presence is not welcome..."

"Oh no, Mr. Grimsby, darling. Please forgive me. I thought you were someone else. Umm. How is your family?"

He was immediately distracted by the question. His face fell into the doleful expression of a basset hound and he began to expound on his mother's ill health, his cheeks wobbling as he talked. Charlotte listened without really listening. Her eyes darted all over the street, expecting to spot the edge of Logan's tailcoat disappearing around a corner.

"But, that is neither here nor there," Mr. Grimsby finished sadly. "Might I walk you to your carriage? Where are your delightful sisters?"

"They're still at home," Charlotte drew herself back into the present by focusing on Mr. Grimsby's watering eyes.

"You didn't come out unaccompanied on a frigid day like this!?" he exclaimed, his second chin leaping from the confines of his scarf in his agitation.

Charlotte shrugged, attempting to calm her racing heart. "I was in need of some air."

"Well," said Mr. Grimsby, looking as though he was torn between admiration and reproach, "we must get you on home."

With that, he held out his arm and hustled her away to his carriage.

CHAPTER FIVE

That hadn't gone at all the way he had hoped.

His left foot throbbed where her heel had connected with his toes, so that he was forced to limp as he made his way down the vacant side streets of Manhattan. Curse her consistent need to strike him. Here he was, hobbling awkwardly over the cobblestones, cradling sore fingers and his injured pride. Curse her.

Logan Drexel was quite accustomed to most of the women he encountered falling at his feet. They were generally enamored by either his good looks or his wealth, and eager to please him.

From their first encounter, he had assumed that Miss Brittler would be just as easy a conquest as any other. He had taken notice of the interest in her eyes, and the jealousy with which she suddenly guarded him and accepted that she would be only too willing to tumble into his arms. But then she had dismissed him.

He had asked for a second dance and she had flounced away from him without a backward glance. He'd been unable to regain her attention for the remainder of the evening.

He had been loath to accept help from his mother, but when she suggested inviting the Brittler women to luncheon, he had grudgingly agreed that this would be as good of a way as any to further his plans. But then Charlotte had stared at him, with those brilliantly green eyes, looking calculating and again... interested. He had opened his mouth and let slide a familiar complement that had brought so many other women to a blush and giggle, and she had drawn back. He had watched her falter.

He let out a groan of frustration. What sort of game was she playing?

He thought for a moment that luck had finally shone upon him when he'd stumbled into Miss Brittler in the street, but... Logan sighed. What a disaster.

He could still see her green eyes turning to steel as he spoke. He could even pinpoint the exact moment he realized he had overstepped, and yet he'd continued spitting out rubbish, digging himself a deeper hole until she had lost her temper and struck. She'd had this defiant, blazing look on her face, as though his words had brushed a deep chord with her. She had been quite beautiful in that moment, like nothing he had ever seen before. Her red hair had come loose from its pins in the wind, and it blew around her face, causing the green in her eyes to gleam momentarily in contrast. He'd paused and swallowed, and in that split second, her heel had slammed onto his foot.

Logan struggled along 52nd Avenue and made his way back onto the High Street. His toes throbbed as he lurched over the threshold of Grunnel's Tavern. It wasn't a particularly classy establishment, but Logan wasn't in the mood for classy.

He plunked himself down at the bar and wrapped his knuckles on the dark wood to signal the bartender. Despite the hour, the place was almost full. The cold weather had driven many a man in search of warmth and comfort. Grunnel's provided both in the way of company, whiskey, and a roaring fire.

At last, with a tall brandy in his hand, Logan felt his various aches began to ease as the tension leaked out of his body.

So much rode on his ability to coerce Charlotte Brittler into a marriage. Everything, really. He wanted to move forward. He needed to, but he needed funds to do that. He intended to pull Drexel Industries out of the deep well of debt and darkness that his father had driven it into. One last deception. One. And he would be free.

"Ye look as though ye've the weight of thee world resting on yer shoulders."

Logan looked up to see who had spoken. A broad-chested Irishman was facing him. He was at least twenty years Logan's senior, and his eyes crinkled pleasantly in the corners. His hair was lank and dark, and his hands were covered with calluses and cracked from hard labor.

Logan eyed the man for a moment, taking in his worn appearance, and then he smiled. "It's not so heavy a world," he said, chuckling.

The Irishman slid across one barstool so that he and Logan were facing one another over the corner of the bar, and he held out his hand. "Roland MacBrady."

Logan took hold of it and shook it, feeling the rough skin against his own. "Logan Drexel."

"Those are some mighty soft hands, Mr. Drexel, if you don't mind my saying." Roland MacBrady smiled to show that the comment was meant as a mere observation, not an insult.

Logan laughed and emptied his glass. "My own private shame," he said wryly, looking at his palms.

"What is weighing so heavily on your fine, young mind?"

Logan waved his hand in dismissal. "Nothing of consequence," he said, sourly. He signaled the bartender for a refill and thanked him when he came with haste.

"Is it money? Or is it a woman?"

Logan looked up from his drink, vaguely surprised, and Roland chuckled.

"Nine times out of ten, when a man sulks and drinks, it's either got to do with money, or it's got to do with a woman."

Logan sat back in his chair, smiling wryly, and loosened the tie that was cutting into his neck. "I suppose this is a bit of both then," he said.

"Can't live without either," shrugged Roland, and he raised his glass in salute to Logan and downed it in one. "If it's a woman, you best be apologizing fast like. It'll do you no good to keep her waitin'. She'll just stew and build the idea up in her mind until you'll be having twice the amount to apologize for."

Logan laughed again. "Perhaps she was in the wrong."

Roland snorted. "Don't make a lick of difference."

Logan lifted his hand and scratched at the thin layer of scruff that was beginning to creep down his neck from his beard, then he sighed. "Her family won't have it," he said, dispassionately. "They disapprove."

"Does she want you?"

That was an interesting question. Did Charlotte Brittler want him? Certainly not after their conversation of a few hours ago. He doubted she would want anything to do with him at all after he'd made a right pig's ear of things.

"I don't know."

"Well, my boy," said Roland, fixing him with a hardened stare, and giving him a knowing nod. "You best be going to find out."

Roland's straight forward explanation made things seem simple, and at the same time, much more complicated. For the first time, Logan was forced to view Charlotte Brittler as a being with emotions and feelings as sharp as his, rather than as a means to an end. He found the idea made his task all the more wearisome. It wasn't as though he intended to marry her and then abandon her. He would make sure she was well cared for...

He couldn't really remember how many he had had as he drained the last dregs of his glass and set it down on the bar. Roland let loose a loud belch from beside him, and Logan chuckled.

"I've no right to intrude on her family's privacy, as you're suggesting."

"A man in love has every right!" shouted Roland, slipping sideways on his stool and tipping beer down his shirt. "Who has better right than you?"

Logan's amusement slipped from his face like sour milk.

Roland, whom he would have thought was beyond noticing anything at that moment, frowned blearily. "You don't love her?"

"Certainly not," said Logan without thinking and Roland glared at him.

"You love her."

"I haven't had the time to love her!" growled Logan.

"Then why court her?!" yelled Roland, loud enough that the whole bar went quiet.

Logan frowned. He was starting to hate himself, and his motives.

"Ahh," whispered his drunken friend, reading his expression. "This is the bit about the money. She's got wealth, has she?"

Logan felt himself sinking into his seat. He looked to Roland, with his calluses and his labor-hardened muscles, and he nodded.

Roland snorted and climbed tipsily from his barstool. "Ain't enough money in the world worth more than the love of a woman," he said.

And with that, he struggled into his coat, tipped his hat, and made his way out the door.

Logan ordered a final round, his frustration balling his hands into fists on the bar in front of him.

The problem was, Roland had been right. A man in love with a woman should try everything in his power to woo her. He could not give up this easily. He did not love Charlotte Brittler, but if he did, he'd have fought for her. He knew that much about himself.

He was quite drunk by now. He paid his tab and floundered across the tavern to the door. Once outside, it took him three tries to whistle for a passing cart. His lips did not seem to want to work properly.

"Where to?" said the driver, peering down at Logan with obvious apprehension.

"Four hunnndred and sixty-two or... perhaps three, Lindbrock Place," slurred Logan. He knew where the

Brittler family house was. Now he'd just have to bribe a footman to discover which window was Charlotte's.

Chapter Six

Charlotte was warm. Wherever she was, heat engulfed her as though she was sitting beside a roaring fire. She rolled over in her sleep. And then there were kisses, feather-light upon her cheeks. Whiskery kisses and she knew without opening her eyes to whom the lips belonged. She felt them wandering over her throat and she moaned, then felt her eyes fly open at the sound.

She sat up straight, clutching the sheets to her chest, and scrambled out of her bed, looking around in the darkness. Her room was empty. Charlotte shivered and then she sighed and, shaking her head, she climbed back into the warmth.

Another dream. They were becoming more and more vivid. She could only hope that she hadn't cried out in her sleep, as she had done the night before. It was dreadful. As though Logan Drexel didn't haunt her thoughts enough while she was awake.

Another small parcel of fury erupted inside her as she recalled her encounter with him earlier today, and she nearly growled. Why? Why was she dreaming about someone she despised? And in such an intimate way. In that half-way place between dreaming and waking, she had been delighted. Excited to have him in her arms. When reality came crashing in, it was invariably disappointing. Until she remembered that she did not even like the man. She should have been relieved.

This obsession was becoming unhealthy. That was exactly what it was, an obsession. She hated him for his presumption and his arrogance, and yet... she ran the tip of her braid through her lips.

There was a tap on her window, and Charlotte looked up, distracted from her sleepy, complicated thoughts. She was on the second story; there were not any trees nearby whose branches should have been able to reach the pane. She stared at the window, waiting, and listening hard. The sound came again, and she had seen it this time. Someone was standing in the yard, tossing pebbles against the glass. She leaped out of bed and hurried across the room, peering down onto the moon-drenched lawn. Her heart leapt into her throat. Yes, there was someone there. It looked like a man. And for one wild moment, Charlotte thought that it was Logan Drexel. Then she recalled how foolish it would be for him to come to her home in the dead of night, and she dismissed the thought as she went in search of her robe.

Locating the thick cotton gown at the end of her bed, she drew it on and went back to the window, trying to locate the figure once more upon the dark landscape. There he was.

But he stood in a myriad of shadows so complete, she couldn't see his face. A little frightened, and wondering if she ought to call for her father, she watched as the figure slid from one patch of shadow to the next, drawing closer to her until he stood right against the house, just beneath her window. She craned her neck to peer down into the flower bed but lost sight of him.

Another pebble struck the window and she jumped. Frowning and feeling as though the world had gone mad, she slipped the catch and slid the frame up so that she could peek down at the stranger.

"Charlotte," the harsh whisper made her heart skip a beat, and she clutched at the neck of her robe, urging her eyes to discern the man's figure from the shadows that surrounded him.

"Miss Brittler? Are you there?"

"Logan?!" she shrieked and then she winced, realizing her mistake.

"Shhhh!" he said hurriedly, and she clapped a hand to her mouth, listening for the telltale squeak of a floorboard that meant that one of her sisters had heard her, and was coming to investigate. There was no sound apart from her terrified breathing.

"What are you doing here?" she hissed.

Logan Drexel took a step back from the house so that he was momentarily awash in moonlight. He smiled, displaying impossibly white teeth. She could make out his thick dark hair and his blue eyes gleaming up at her out of the darkness. He looked pale and sickeningly handsome in the moonlight, and she glared at him.

"Go away," she said, and she made to close the window.

"Wait," he breathed, and Charlotte hesitated, despite herself. "I've come to apologize."

Charlotte felt shock flit over her features. Logan took advantage of her silence.

"I behaved like a pig-headed- "

"Yes, you did," she interrupted him. "And now I would like you to leave."

"But I-" Logan Drexel took another step backward and stumbled, and Charlotte was seized by a sudden thought.

"Mister Drexel, are you drunk?"

His cheeks colored at her words, and he let loose a quiet, little belch. "That is neither here nor there," he said, waving a hand nonchalantly. "I've come to make things right between us."

"There is nothing between us to correct, Mister Drexel. Kindly remove yourself from my father's property before I make your presence here known to all."

"Shhhppp, don't do that," giggled Logan. With that, he plopped his body down onto the dew-spotted grass and gazed up at her imploringly. "I hoped we might 'ave a little chat."

"We'll do nothing of the sort," she growled. "Go away," she made to close the window again.

"I didn't mean the things I said," continued Logan, as though he hadn't heard her. "I know you're not like those other ones. You've got a mind of your own, arnd it was quite wrong of me to suggest otherwise."

"Yes, it was, Mister Drexel. But if you do not cease to occupy the space below my window, I will never forgive you for it. Go away."

"I cannot leave until you tell me you have forgiven me," stated Logan stubbornly. He looked absurd, sitting there on the lawn in the darkness. His legs were splayed out in front of him as though he did not have a care in the world, and he looked up at her with the utmost mischief in his eyes. "I could sing if you like," he suggested mildly. "Would that make you happy?"

"Certainly not!" squeaked Charlotte, glancing around the yard. What would the servants think if they saw him there? What would her father do if he discovered Logan Drexel had come to visit her in the dead of night?

To her absolute horror, Logan threw his head back and began to sing, his voice jarring in the silence.

"There once was a lass who stole my heart! Diddly-diddly doo! There once was a lass who stole my heart, and my darling Charlotte, 'twas you!!!"

He was utterly sauced. Charlotte dithered on the spot, unsure what to do, but if he kept singing like that, he was bound to wake the whole house!

"Shh! Mr. Drexel, shut up!"

"I cannot, Miss!" laughed Logan, all thought of secrecy forgotten. "You must forgive me!"

He began to sing again.

Terrified, Charlotte snatched a heavy vase off her vanity and hurled it out the window. It landed, right on target, on the top of Logan's head. His verse halted abruptly and he crumpled to the ground.

Charlotte sighed in relief, listening to her heart thundering in her ears, and then panic began to set in. He was out cold. Now what was she going to do? She couldn't just leave him there until dawn; what if someone found him before he woke?

Charlotte slid the window closed, her heart hammering in her chest. She had to get him home, but how on Earth was she going to do that without help?

Kincaid. Yes. If she had to have help, the footman, Kincaid was the most likely to accept a bribe for his silence. She pulled on her slippers and tiptoed downstairs.

She found the footman in the servants' hall. His hair was disheveled, and he had a cigar clamped between his thin lips. He was whistling softly through his teeth and looking heartily pleased about something. It was a stroke of luck that no one else was about.

"Kincaid."

The footman stood up so suddenly, he looked as though someone had pricked him with a pin.

"Miss Brittler? What are you doing down here?"

"Kincaid, I need your help."

Together, Charlotte and the footman dragged Logan Drexel's limp body into the carriage that they found parked at the end of the street. The driver was snoozing soundly and not at all pleased to be woken.

"What've yer done to him?" he asked confusedly as he jumped from the cart to assist them in heaving Mister Drexel into the carriage.

"Never you mind," said Charlotte sternly. "Take him to Drexel Manor." She stuffed a wad of bills into the cabby's hand and darted into the carriage to reassure herself—for the fifth time— that she had not killed the man.

There was a sizable lump forming on the top of his head, but other than that, he looked alright. She gave his face a gentle slap, and his eyelids fluttered.

"You fool," she said dispassionately. She climbed out of the carriage. Kincaid was talking quietly with the driver. She had a feeling he was ensuring the man's silence. Whatever his other faults, Kincaid was nothing if not thorough.

"You best be off with him."

The driver tilted his cap as Charlotte slammed the carriage door. With a slap of the reins, Logan Drexel was going, going… gone.

"What a dreadful thing, Miss," said Kincaid, shaking his head. "The fellow didn't seem so bad when he asked for your window. Thought he might be your fancy-man."

"You told him which window was mine?"

Kincaid looked uncomfortable. He grinned shiftily. "Clearly, I was wrong."

"Kincaid, if you hadn't just helped me out of a very tight spot, I assure you, I'd be very angry." Charlotte yawned. "But, I'm afraid I'm just too tired to care much at the moment."

Going down to breakfast the next morning was a trial. She pleaded for Penny to leave her to rest.

"Just tell mother I'm not well," she begged the maid.

"I think she'd storm up here and yank you out of bed herself, miss. Today's the auction on Staten Island. I don't think she'll let you miss it."

Charlotte fell back onto her pillows with a groan and covered her face with her hands.

The auction. How had she forgotten? Well, naturally, last night's excitement would have driven it clean out of her mind. Six hours of listening to an auctioneer shouting continuously into a speaking trumpet was not her idea of a good time. Especially after a night of little to no sleep. Nor did she have any desire to watch her mother and father's wealthy friends bid on overpriced pieces that, in her opinion, had little artistic value.

Many of her friends and acquaintances had just as much talent in the way of painting or sculpture as the artists whose pieces they would all be bidding on today. And her mother had horrid taste in decoration. She was likely to choose a bland, unremarkable still-life that depicted a bowl of fruit.

With an irritated grumble, Charlotte flung away the coverlet and started to get dressed.

She perked up a bit as they entered McGeerson's auction house off Femmingway. Spotting familiar faces in the crowd, she made her way over to the refreshments table and then joined her friends, Noelle tagging along behind her. Sarah-Jane had immersed herself in conversation with a well-to-do wool merchant and looked as though she would not be surfacing for several minutes yet.

In a trice, Mrs. Brittler had wheedled her way into an acquaintance with Marcellus Hartley, the noted arms dealer, and his wife. She was bobbing and curtsying with an almost unseemly enthusiasm, as she was bound to do when in the presence of distinct wealth. Thomas Brittler was having to hold firm to her arm to prevent his wife from escaping.

"Charlotte! Noelle! My dears, where have you been hiding?"

A stalky brunette with a heart-shaped face stood to greet the two Brittler sisters. She had been chatting obligingly with a tall, leggy blonde in a pale green dress that clung to her form just enough to make it enticing to the gentlemen, but not enough for the matrons in the crowd to whisper behind their gloves.

Anna, the brunette, had taken Charlotte's hand into her own, beaming fondly. Charlotte returned her smile with equal ardor. "Anna," she cooed, kissing her friend on each cheek. "It's so wonderful to see you. I thought you said you weren't planning to attend."

"I wasn't," growled Anna Sloan, casting a wary look towards her father, who was holding court in the upper right-hand corner of the arranged seats, his bald pate gleaming as he laughed jovially. "Papa had other ideas."

"So I see," whispered Charlotte, watching as Professor Sloan bent his ear to a woman that looked much too young for him.

Anna rolled her eyes and gestured to the blonde she had been chatting with earlier. "Ladies, this is Emma Hartley. Her father is the owner of Remington Arms."

"Of course," said Charlotte, offering her hand to the woman. "Charlotte Brittler, Miss Hartley, and this is my sister, Noelle."

Emma Hartley shook Charlotte's hand and then Noelle's with a certain amount of calculation in her gaze. She was pretty, no doubt, but she also had a certain air of vanity and presumption about her that Charlotte couldn't manage to find pleasing. As she settled into a seat beside her friend, she decided to reserve judgment on Miss Hartley.

The auctioneer stepped onto the podium and began shuffling papers. He was speaking to a thin chap about Charlotte's age, who nodded and began chivvying the other attendees into their seats. One by one, the attendant handed out paddles and marked them on his clipboard and a moment later, the bidding started.

Charlotte fanned herself idly with her paddle, doing her best to tune out the auctioneer's deafening gibberish. She eyed the pieces on display around the walls, and when that failed to hold her attention, she watched the crowd.

Her mother was whispering to her father. Mathew Griggs was bouncing his knee agitatedly. A few seats in front of Charlotte and a little to the left, she could make out sweet Mr. Grimsby, who was sweating profusely in his place next to a woman in a dangerously low-cut dress. At that moment, the woman turned her face to take a sip of her punch, and Charlotte had to grapple with a sudden thrill of loathing. Eliza Carlisle. Charlotte felt her upper lip curl in distaste. No wonder Mr. Grimsby was looking so agitated. What man in his right mind would be able to ignore that disgraceful exhibition?

A deep, masculine chuckle from her right made Charlotte look around. She was surprised that she could hear anything over the sound of the auctioneer and his insufferable gavel.

Her breath hitched. Two seats along, his face split in an arrogant smirk that befitted the devil himself, sat Logan Drexel. He was not looking at her, but she knew without a doubt, that it had been he who had laughed, and—knowing the reason for his amusement—she was half-tempted to reach across her sister and knock his gleaming top hat to the floor.

Her tongue glued itself to the roof of her mouth as she bit back the furious diatribe she longed to cast forth. What was he doing here? Perhaps she hadn't clobbered him hard enough with that vase. He shouldn't be able to walk this afternoon, let alone attend an auction. His head had to be pounding.

Charlotte felt an evil sense of delight at this thought. Yes, indeed, for all the suffering and irritation Logan Drexel was putting her through, she hoped his head was hurting rather horribly indeed.

The auctioneer had drawn to a halt. He was now accepting a glass of water from his assistant, and the crowd was beginning to talk amongst themselves once more. Charlotte welcomed the brief respite.

"Isn't it just gorgeous?" sighed Anna from next to her, and she took hold of Charlotte's wrist. "I've never seen anything quite like it."

Charlotte turned her gaze to the stand and knew exactly what her friend was talking about.

Resplendent in a gilded frame, the painting was illuminated beneath the bright sunlight that filtered in through the skylights over their heads. For the second time that hour, Charlotte felt her breath seize in her chest.

The artist had taken such painstaking efforts to capture the profile of his subject that the end effect was quite marvelous. Her hair was like fire. It flowed around her shoulders and down the back of a loose-laced, golden gown. She had been turned away when he had painted her, or perhaps the artist had wanted to retain his model's identity for himself. Whatever the reason, only her shoulder and back were visible. The rest of her was hidden in her brilliant, red curls.

Charlotte had never seen anything so awe inspiring.

"She looks like you," giggled Noelle.

Charlotte blushed. "Not every woman with red hair is me, 'Elle."

"No, she's right," countered Anna, now looking quizzically back and forth between Charlotte and the painting. "She looks just like you. The hair is perfect."

"That woman," said Charlotte fiercely, getting to her feet and sliding up the space between the chairs, "has nothing in common with me apart from the fact that she has red hair. Look at her, she's..." but Charlotte trailed off because she had been interrupted by a whisper in her ear.

"Beautiful," said Logan Drexel as he stood up to make room for her. His words were so low that Charlotte knew they were meant for her alone. She felt his hot breath brush the back of her neck as he said them. "Absolutely beautiful."

Charlotte caught Logan's eye, and time stopped. Neither of them moved, and the noise and bustle of the room fell away. Charlotte felt fire leap to life in her chest, and in that frozen second, she fell in love.

Chapter Seven

His fingers twitched as he suppressed the urge to reach for her. Didn't she know how the world saw her? Didn't she know how beautiful she was? He collapsed back into his seat after she passed him, breathing deeply, trying to calm himself.

His eyes darted around the auction hall, and he caught sight of Miss Carlisle. She was eyeing him, and after a second, she offered him a coy "come-hither." He shook his head almost imperceptibly and tried not to watch her face fall in disappointment.

He closed his eyes, his head throbbing. He'd come here with two tasks in mind. Two desperate, complicated tasks that, unless carried out, would make his plans for Charlotte Brittler all the more difficult.

The first was because of the painting. As one of the many artists represented in today's auction, he was obliged to see it through until the end. He was also very curious to see how his work would be received. He'd sold a couple pieces here and there to supplement his father's difficult gambling habits, but never had he been so invested in the outcome. Who would have her? Who would have the portrait of the flaming haired woman that was beginning to haunt every dark and forsaken corner of his imagination?

For some reason that he could not begin to fathom, Logan was suddenly having difficulty with the idea of some other man owning the painting that he had put so much of his soul into. He had begun the project as a trick, as a means to an end, before he had ever met Charlotte. He'd thought that if he displayed his work here, where she could see, she might soften to him, perhaps even pursue him, taking much of the effort out of the burden of courting her. But with each of his encounters with her, the painting had taken on more life, more substance. It had become her. No longer a figment of his over-active imagination. But really, truly, Charlotte.

The auctioneer was back on the stand, calling for silence. Charlotte had not returned from wherever she had gone.

"This charming piece was donated by one of our members," said the auctioneer smoothly. "The artist prefers to remain anonymous."

A ripple of whispers flooded through the hall at these words as gossips—old and young—turned to one another and began drawing conclusions as to who the woman in the painting could be.

"Ahhem," the auctioneer cleared his throat and continued. "We'll start the bidding at one hundred dollars. Do I hear one- one hundred to Miss Bradshaw. Do I hear one-twenty?"

Logan watched in mounting astonishment as the bids grew higher until the auctioneer was dancing a jig on the podium to keep up. "Four hundred US dollars. Do I hear four-fifty?"

"Six hundred!" A balding, sweating man in a pinstriped suit at least five years out of fashion had stood up and waved his paddle wildly in the air. Logan's nose wrinkled. Not this one. Someone else, please.

The auctioneer's eyes had gone wide. He swallowed. "Alright, six hundred. Do I hear six-fifty?"

"Seven hundred."

The speaker was Miss Carlisle. Logan nearly buried his face in his hands.

"Seven twenty," said the sweating man, looking indignant.

"Eight." Logan did not know what made him say it. In fact, for a moment, he thought someone else had called out, and he looked wildly around the room for the speaker.

"Nine," Miss Carlisle's voice had risen in pitch. She sounded like a buckled shoe squeaking on a polished marble floor.

Logan stared at the painting on the stand, remembering every brush stroke and every fantasy that had come with them. Then he shook his head and sat back down. He would have to let her go.

The auctioneer was looking to Mister Sweaty-Face. "Nine hundred going once? Nine hundred going twice?"

Sweaty-Face raised his paddle in a defeated sort of way. "One thousand," he said miserably.

Miss Carlisle sputtered. The auctioneer was staring her, his gavel suspended in the air. She frowned hard at the painting, then, with a sigh, she sat back down.

The gavel descended.

"Sold to Mister Grimsby of Manhattan, for one thousand US dollars."

CHARLOTTE

Mister Grimsby was shaking hands all around, patting his sweating brow with a yellowed kerchief as he did so. Then he walked up to the podium to speak with the assistant while Logan's painting was removed from the stand.

Logan watched her go with his heart aching in a hollow sort of way, as though he truly had just sold a part of his soul for the sum of one thousand dollars.

His blood still pounding from the enormity of his decision, he sat through the remainder of the auction in sour-faced silence. He should be pleased. One thousand dollars. He'd never even dreamed that Charlotte's abstract profile would have fetched so much, not painted with his clumsy hand. Of course, he himself would have paid that much for it and more.

Logan would be lying to himself if he tried to claim that he saw no beauty in the piece. It had been a turning stone in his work. Already, he had started on another. But he had thought his love for the painting was in its creation, a sort of "beauty in the eye of the beholder." But there had been no mistaking the whispers that had accompanied its reveal on the platform. Evidently, he was not the only person who thought Charlotte Brittler an elegant creature of fascination.

Speaking of Charlotte... he craned his neck—trying to look as though he was merely stretching—and glanced around the room for her. She had still not returned. Blast. So, she hadn't even seen the bidding for her portrait. Where had she gone?

An ominous feeling settled over Logan, and he stood up so suddenly that he knocked the drink from his neighbor's hand. Muttering an apology, he streaked up the aisle between the chairs and darted out into the gallery. There was no one there.

The long, wood-paneled hall was lined with paintings, sculptures and variously unrecognizable objects. There were five doors leading out. One of them, Logan knew, was the entrance to the auction house. The double doors were always snapped shut when an auction began.

The second lead to the main office. Logan had visited here when he had inquired with the keeper of the auction house about selling his work.

He had never been through any of the other doors. Resisting the urge to yank each open and shout Charlotte's name, he approached the first quietly and pressed his ear to it.

The tinkling sound of music echoed back to him, dulled by the thick wood. Frowning in confusion, he pressed his ear still more firmly against the door. Someone inside this room was playing the pianoforte? Trying not to make a sound—although not quite sure why— Logan reached for the handle and opened the door. It swung open noiselessly, and the sight that greeted him made his chest constrict.

Bright winter sunlight was dancing across a room packed with mismatched artifacts. Some in boxes and crates, some with canvas cloths flung across them. A few painted landscapes sat uncovered against the high, mullion windows.

Clouds of dust swirled in the shafts of light, making the room sparkle. And in the center of all the chaos, there she sat. Her red hair was piled on the top of her head, not cascading down her back, as it had been in his painting, and she looked entranced. Her fingers worked magically over the keys, producing a melody of such haunting beauty and intimacy, he felt almost as though he had surprised her in the act of dressing.

For a moment, Logan thought he might have stepped into a dream. Her music flowed over him, encasing him in a gossamer web. The world had gone, there was nothing but this woman, and the swell of her chest as she breathed in time with the music she was creating; the curve of her hips as she sat on an enameled bench, her small feet working the pedals of the piano.

He took a step closer to her, wanting to see her face illuminated in winter sunlight.

Her eyes were closed. If not for the gentle sway of her body as she breathed, he would have thought she had fallen asleep.

He had to get closer to her.

Logan took another step, but as he moved, his foot caught the corner of an open crate that he hadn't noticed sitting at his feet. With a bellowed oath, he felt himself pitch sideways into the stack of boxes next to him.

The music halted and he looked up to see Charlotte leaping from the piano bench, her mouth agape.

Boxes toppled to the floor around him, and Logan bent to catch an ornate floral-patterned pot before it shattered on the floor.

"Mister Drexel! What in Heaven's name are you...?"

"I noticed you hadn't returned," he said quickly, holding up his hands in case she decided to take yet another swing at him. "I came to check on you."

Charlotte's slender fingers found her hips and she looked furious. Why did she always look at him as though he were something vile she had found stuck to the bottom of her boot?

"Mister Drexel." She repeated his name slowly, as though she were speaking to someone very slow and possibly deaf. "I have made it very clear, in my opinion, that your concern is not warranted, nor is it welcomed. You, however, seem to cherish a distinct inability to understand when your very presence is not welcome."

"I only worried that you might have... fallen ill, or..." why had he been so worried for her? Could she not have simply slipped out for some air? He swallowed.

"Disregarding the fact that my health and well-being have absolutely no bearing in your own peace of mind, why did you feel it necessary to skulk in the doorway and spy on me?"

Logan felt himself recovering rapidly. She was setting his teeth on edge. "I thought it strange that someone should trespass on the private collections while the auctioneer was otherwise engaged. Surely, you must be aware that this room is off limits?"

She flushed, and Logan felt a wicked sense of satisfaction. He'd ruffled her.

"I hoped this door would take me onto the side road..."

"And when it became evident it would not?"

Her color deepened. "I..." she gestured wordlessly to the pianoforte behind her. "I only wanted..." she straightened. "I do not see how what I do or do not do is any of your business at all," she stated. "I can't see why you continue to press your company on me when..."

Logan sighed irritably. "Very well," he huffed, and he turned to go, but he had only gone two paces before he turned back to her. "Why?" he demanded without rancor. "Why do you suddenly find me so repellant?"

"Suddenly?" Her responding laugh was high and cold. "In the brief time that I have been in your acquaintance, you have managed to embarrass me on multiple occasions, and last night..." she trailed off disbelievingly, her lips pursed. "How is your head?"

"It hurts rather a lot, thank you for asking." He glared at her and removed his top hat to reveal the jagged cut that ran just above his hairline. "Was that really necessary?"

She looked affronted and a little disgusted. "Of course it was. Your presence would have brought all sorts of trouble down on my family had you been discovered."

He snorted. "You haven't answered my question."

"Yes, I have. Now, if you don't mind," she bent and pulled a displaced canvas cover over the piano. "I would like to get back to the auction."

Just then, the sounds of chattering, the grinding of seats being pushed back, and the tapping of footsteps announced the auction's end. People were flooding into the hall.

Logan looked down and was surprised to see that he still held the floral pot in his hands. Replacing it hastily on the top of a nearby box, he offered Charlotte his elbow.

"Here," he said, "we can blend into the crowd."

But Charlotte's eyes had grown wide, she took a step forward, but before Logan had looked around, the pot had tumbled from its precarious perch and shattered on the marble floor.

"Who's there?!" Logan recognized the voice of the auctioneer and heard running footsteps coming towards them.

"Quick!" hissed Logan, and he took Charlotte by the arm and steered her out of sight behind a tall sculpture. The auctioneer entered the room just as Charlotte's silken blue skirt had whipped around the corner. Logan pulled her tight against his chest and slid them both beneath the sculpture's billowing sheet.

"I said, who's there? You're not supposed to be-" Logan heard the crunch of pottery. The auctioneer had trodden on the broken pot. "What the-?" He cursed and

Logan heard the door slam and the sound of a key turning in the lock.

"What are we going to do?!" squeaked Charlotte as soon as he'd gone. "If we're discovered…"

Logan was thinking fast. "The window," he whispered. "Quickly!"

Charlotte tossed the canvas off their heads and they made a beeline for the mullion windows at the far end of the room.

"Locked," he said, fumbling with the frame of the first.

"This one's open," Charlotte had moved to the furthest window and slid the catch. She poked her head out. "It's too far to jump!"

"Nonsense," whispered Logan. He stuck his head out the window and peered out into the back alley behind the auction house. "I'll lower you down first."

"Oh, but-!"

"Now! Before he comes back!"

Charlotte nodded. "Don't drop me."

"I might just," he chuckled. "I owe you a knock on the head."

She glared at him, then hoisted herself onto the ledge and shimmied out the window. He took a half-second to admire the unprecedented agility with which she moved and then took hold of her hands. Anchoring himself on the ledge, he lowered her until she was only a foot or so off the ground.

"Ready?"

"Yes, hurry!"

He let go. She landed gracefully, with little more than a wince, and he lifted himself back into the window so that he could come out feet first. At that moment, the door handle rattled. He could hear the irritable voice of the auctioneer grousing at his assistant. "The door is to be locked every time, Creswell. Somebody's been in here. I think I locked them in."

The door handle turned, but Logan had already jumped.

He landed hard on his feet and it felt as though his legs would shatter. He toppled over on his backside for a moment, and then Charlotte was there. She tugged at his hands and pulled him to his feet.

"Run!" she giggled, and Logan stumbled, astounded to see that she was smiling. "Run!" she said again. Without pausing to think, he took hold of her hand and ran.

They darted through a maze of alleys and side streets, Charlotte's light blue skirts swishing as he pulled her onward. At last, they collapsed, breathing heavily, against the brick wall of a fish house. The stench was unbelievable, but Charlotte was still smiling. He looked at her, shocked, and when she met his eyes, her chest heaving, she threw back her head and laughed to the sky.

"What in the blazes is so funny?!" he growled. He was still holding her gloved hand in his, but he tossed it away from him in his agitation.

"Oh, my. That was quite a rush, wasn't it?"

"Do you realize what the consequences would have been if they'd have caught us? We're lucky to have escaped. Our reputations would have been ruined. We'd have been brought before the judge. I bet that vase was worth four hundred dollars."

Charlotte huffed in amusement. "You do seem to have difficulty with them."

Logan scowled at her. "Only when I'm in your presence, my dear."

"I'm not 'your dear,'" she said, with an abrupt return to her normal state of annoyance. Although, the laughter had not quite faded from her eyes. "And you best be remembering that."

"It was a figure of speech," Logan sighed, goaded past endurance. "Come, your family will be missing you." He offered her his arm again, but she didn't take it.

"It's time I was plain with you," she said. Over their heads a seagull circled, screaming out the horrid music of its kin.

"Oh?"

"Mister Drexel, I enjoy your company. While I find your arrogance abhorrent and your manners disdainful," he raised his eyebrows at this. "I find that I am interested in pursuing a bit of excitement."

His heart gave a leap, and he felt a small, hopeful bubble burgeon in his stomach. He grinned at her. "Excitement, eh? Would my person be considered enough excitement for one such as yourself?"

He reached for her, but she held up a hand to stop him. "Unfortunately," she said, and he groaned as she said it. "My father has threatened to disinherit me if I so much as breath in your delightful," she rolled her eyes on that word, "presence."

Being struck by a lightning bolt must be something like this, he thought. A furious jolt had gone through him at her words, and his mind had filled with a sort of blank buzzing. She was still talking.

"I don't want to give you the impression that I am wholly controlled by the will of others... but I must be able to manage. So," she fixed him with a business-like gaze, "if you wish to pursue an acquaintance with me, I encourage you to first win my father's approval. Good day to you."

And she left him standing there, with nothing but the smell of stinking fish and the cries of the gulls screeching overhead. He watched her walk away from him with a steady self-revulsion growing in the pit of his stomach. A bird dropping landed on his shoulder.

As Charlotte's demure form slunk around a corner and out of sight, she cast him a taunting smile. When she was gone, Logan seized a rock from the ground and hurled it at the gulls. Their hideous cries of laughter followed him as departed the scene.

Chapter Eight

A HUM OF EXCITED chatter met Charlotte's ears as she rejoined her family on the front steps of the auction house.

"What's going on?" she asked Sarah-Jane as she drew closer to them.

"Charlotte, there you are. Where have you been? Never mind. Someone tried to rob the auction hall!"

"When?" ask Charlotte, nonplussed.

"While we were there!"

Charlotte rolled her eyes. Of course, the gossips of New York would work up a smashed pot into something sinister. That's what they were best at. She noticed Logan Drexel return to the crowd as well, coming from the opposite direction that she had. He did not look at her.

People milled about, chatting excitedly until rain began to fall on all their heads. In groups of two and three, the high society of New York stepped into their carriages and trundled off towards home. Charlotte's cheeks were still warm.

"Are you sure you're feeling alright?" asked Noelle for the second time, pressing her cold fingers to Charlotte's head. "You look awfully gray, you know."

"Perhaps you should lie down when we get home," chimed her mother, and Charlotte agreed. She needed time to think.

By the time they reached the house, she was sweating. Her hands were clammy and cold. She was, after all, feeling a little ill.

She went upstairs to bed and rang for Penny to bring her a cup of hot tea.

What an adventure she'd had today. Charlotte wasn't used to such excitement. She undressed slowly and sank into the down comforter with a newfound sense of purpose.

Charlotte Brittler wasn't one to go looking for trouble. She never had. She was good with rules, regulations, and propriety. She knew right from wrong. Her behavior today had been shameful, but the worst part of all was that she felt completely unrepentant. In fact, Charlotte thought, as she snuggled down into her bed for some much-needed rest, after the fun of today's grand adventure, she was quite keen to have another one.

⁓

The following days were filled with a monotony so consuming that Charlotte found it very difficult to settle to anything. Five days after the auction found her in the kitchen, alongside Noelle, who was kneading bread dough with an intense fervor.

"You need a hobby," said Noelle, shoving a bowl into her hands. "Sprinkle some flour on here for me. A little more. A little more. That's good."

"You think I should take up flour sprinkling?" muttered Charlotte dryly, replacing the bowl on the draining board.

"I think you need something to occupy your mind," said her sister wisely. She swiped at a strand of blonde hair that continued to fall over her eyes, leaving a streak of flour across her forehead.

"Is that why you bake?"

"I bake because I want to, yes. I enjoy it, and it gives Marcia a break." Noelle leaned around her sister for the rolling pin. "You could help, you know."

"I thought I was helping," laughed Charlotte.

"You're moping," responded Noelle with a roll of her eyes. "Moping doesn't help anyone."

"I'm not moping!" said Charlotte indignantly.

At this, Noelle spun around and pointed the floury rolling pin threateningly at Charlotte's chest. "Sometimes, dear sister, you seem to forget who you're talking to. I saw your face that night."

"Which night?"

"The night of the Drexel's ball. I saw how you looked at Logan Drexel."

"I don't know what you're talking about," protested Charlotte. She took a step back from her sister and sank down on one of the barstools.

"There you go again!" squalled Noelle. She seized a handful of loose flour and tossed it on top of Charlotte's head.

"No-elle!"

"Fess up!" laughed her sister, grabbing another handful of flour. Charlotte put her arms up to defend herself.

"I can't confess to something that isn't true."

Splat! Charlotte was pretty sure a chunk of dough had come with the flour that time. "Noelle! Stop!"

But her sister reached for the flour once more. Giggling like a mad woman she rushed Charlotte with the ferocity of an angry boar. Charlotte dodged around the handfuls of flour and ran for the counter.

"Stand back!" she said, now with two handfuls of her own.

Noelle was still grinning. "Admit it. You've fallen for him. I was right there when you walked past him at the auction last weekend. I saw the way he looked at you!"

"Noelle, Logan Drexel is out of bounds. Father said—"

"Change his mind," whispered Noelle. Ever the romantic, her sister relaxed and sank onto Charlotte's recently vacated barstool with a dreamy look in her eye. Flour leaked out of her closed fists and dusted the stone floor. "If a man looked at me the way Logan Drexel looked at you just then, I'd fight for him. You mark my words. When a man like that comes along for me, I'll run away with him before I let anyone tell me I can't have him." There was such a fierce look in her eye that, for a moment, Charlotte actually believed her.

She awoke the next day with a plan fully formed in her mind, as though her brain had been operating at full force while she slept. Her father, Thomas Brittler, appreciated a man with honor and integrity. If Berkley Drexel, Logan's father, had stolen Dianna's dowry, surely Logan had a way of finding out.

What if Logan came to visit Thomas at his office in town? What if he replaced the money his father had stolen? Surely, surely, that would cleanse Logan in her father's eyes? In any case, it might at least make their... friendship—for lack of a better word—more acceptable to him.

Delighted with herself, Charlotte flew out of bed and started to get dressed.

An hour later, the carriage trundled to a halt in front of Drexel manor, and Charlotte mounted the steep steps with a certain amount of trepidation. Before she had even raised her fist to knock, however, the door was pulled open by the surly-faced butler she had met on her second visit to Drexel manor.

"Mister Drexel is waiting for you in the parlor."

"Thank you."

Charlotte lifted her skirts and stepped into the cavernous foyer. The butler closed the door with a snap and gestured to the room immediately on her left.

She slipped inside without waiting to be introduced and said boldly:

"I've had an idea."

Logan Drexel had been sitting upright on a luridly floral settee—something her mother would have no doubt appreciated— raising a steaming cup of coffee to his lips. He jolted as she entered and raised an eyebrow, wiping at the fresh stain on his shirtfront.

"Miss Brittler," he muttered as he stood, setting down his coffee and retrieving a cloth napkin from the side table. "I didn't expect to be seeing you again so soon, much less," he coughed, "in my parlor room."

"Your mother bid me visit if I felt so inclined," she said, looking around. She had never been in this room before.

The parlor was decorated in the same sumptuous manner as the rest of the house, designed to raise jealousy and envy in anyone who entered.

"Has it occurred to you that your driver might mention your visit to your father?" Logan inquired.

Charlotte waved her hand dismissively. "I've got Kincaid with me today, his loyalty is for hire. He's taking me to the shops this morning for a new set of ink pens."

Logan frowned as though the name was familiar to him. "Was he the footman who-?"

"Helped me attend to your drunken self the other night? Yes, that's him."

"Good man," said Logan.

"For a price," muttered Charlotte. She wandered across the room, examining the small bookcase. It looked a bit ruffled. Books were stuck into slots haphazardly, as though the reader had discarded them alternately when they failed to distract. Charlotte wondered why the maid had not been in to tidy them up. She turned back to Logan.

"You have given me the impression on multiple occasions that you wish to court me. I assume that your main interest lies in the portion of my inheritance that I will receive upon my making a suitable marriage," Logan coughed as she said this, but she avoided his eye. She had to be straight with him. "I will not marry without love."

She could feel his eyes following her as she made her way around the room, and they put her in mind of a cat stalking a mouse. "If you still wish to court me, I've come up with a plan that may enable you to come into my father's good graces. If you are still interested, I will discuss the matter with you further, after I have laid out a few conditions."

"Conditions?"

She chanced a glance at him. He was staring at her as though he had never seen anything like her before. He looked incredulous. It was not an altogether reassuring expression.

"Are you still interested?"

Logan swallowed. "I..."

This split-second hesitation was enough to cast doubt on Charlotte's whole façade.

"Yes, of course I am." He took a step towards her, but Charlotte crossed the room and then turned to face him. Her gaze was hard. She was sizing him up. Was this man worth the effort? Would a man like Logan Drexel offer her a happy future? Would he offer her love?

Charlotte sighed and looked away from him, now examining the draperies—which were a little dusty. She had decided she would give him the chance to win her heart. Decided she would take a little risk. But... her conditions. Yes.

"If my plan succeeds, I would like to reserve the right to end our courtship at any time. I will not be held as a prisoner or a keepsake. If I find that we are not suited, we will part. We will end it smoothly, without fuss or gossip."

Logan's left brow had crept up towards his hairline. "Of course," he agreed, as though this was obvious.

Charlotte held up two fingers. "Secondly, I will not be pressured into a marriage with you. If you, or anyone else, for that matter, attempts to do so, I will terminate our courtship."

Logan looked as though he was about to protest. "Surely you do not wish to make me responsible for the behavior of others?"

"Thirdly," said Charlotte, as though Logan had not uttered. "You will not touch me."

Logan had gone to take a mouthful of coffee, as though to steady himself, but as she said these last words, the coffee came flooding out of his mouth. He coughed again.

"Hot coffee," he whispered, reaching for his napkin to mop up his mess. "You expect me to determine whether I would like to spend the rest of my life with you without ever having touched you?"

Charlotte blushed as she tried to explain. "I have difficulty...functioning properly... when you are near me. The feeling gets worse when you touch me. If I am expected to make an informed and logical decision about our future together, I will need to be in full control of my emotions."

"I see."

Logan did not speak for a long while, and Charlotte resumed her examination of the draperies.

"You're very unusual, Miss Brittler."

She looked up and was surprised to see that he had slunk closer to her while she'd been looking the other way. She could feel the heat of him warming the air as he approached, and she had a sudden, vivid flashback of his hands on her waist. He had pulled her so close to him at the auction house the other day. She had thought she might faint with the feel of him against her as they hid beneath the canvas.

She exhaled violently and moved away from him. To her dismay, he followed her. She sank down on the settee, and he did the same on the opposite end, still looking at her.

"Very well," he said. "You reserve the right to end our courtship for any reason. You will not be pressured into a marriage, and I will not," he winced as though the words were sharp on his tongue, "touch you during the term of our courtship."

Charlotte gave a short little nod, and Logan held out his hand as though they were striking a bargain. Charlotte glared at him pointedly.

"Technically, our courtship has not yet begun," he said, by way of an explanation. Charlotte frowned. She hadn't thought of this. Logan's responding smile was almost too innocent.

She took his hand and shook it, breaking the contact quickly. Logan's grin grew wider still.

"If—and only if—you are able to gain my father's approval, I will ensure that my mother issues you with an invitation to join us for dinner. Our courtship will officially begin at that time."

Logan nodded. "What is your plan?"

It was Charlotte's turn to hesitate. "...I'm afraid it concerns some rather sensitive subject material."

"Indeed?"

"Yes. And I'd urge you not to repeat this. Not to anyone."

"Really?" Logan's curiosity was evidently piqued. He'd turned his entire body to face her now.

Charlotte took a breath. "My father is under the impression that, through his various business dealings, your father somehow robbed my family of Dianna's portion of inheritance. Her dowry. Is it true?"

Logan's face went pale. "Frankly, I rather resent the accusation," he said.

"Can you tell me that it's not? That my father is mistaken?"

Logan tugged at the neck of his coffee stained shirt front, apparently to give himself thinking time. "I don't-"

"But you could find out," interrupted Charlotte.

"I-" Logan sighed. "Unfortunately," he said, lowering his voice, although there was no one around to hear. "Your father is very likely correct."

"You must be joking," said Charlotte, astounded. She had expected him to deny it. To shoot her idea down. Or pretend to play along but never admit his father's guilt.

But Logan was shaking his head. "What do you propose we do about it?"

"Give the money back," said Charlotte. It seemed the most obvious thing in the world to her.

Logan sat in silence for a full minute, his face completely expressionless. Then, so suddenly that it made her jump, he let out peal of bark-like laughter.

"Miss Brittler, how do you suppose I go about doing that?"

Charlotte looked around the sumptuous parlor, her expression plain, and Logan laughed again.

He crossed to the window and ran a finger over the sill, lifting it to display the thick streak of dust and residue it gathered. "This house is a sham. The company is about to drown. My father has spent and wasted and destroyed everything we ever had. I could no more repay your father than cut off one of my limbs."

Charlotte gaped at him. "It's...It's true then?"

"That my family's reputation is built on the lies of my father?" He gave a great sigh, his chest heaving. "Not exactly. My grandfather built this company. He made Drexel Industries what it used to be. My father sold it off, bit by bit, until there was nothing left. What he didn't sell, he gambled away. When the money ran out, he began resorting to crude and illegal schemes to pay off his debts."

Charlotte felt the shock of these words reverberate in the air, not quite knowing what to say.

"We'll find a way," she whispered after a moment. "If this is what you want... we'll find a way."

Chapter Nine

Logan stared after Charlotte's carriage as it retreated down the rain-swept drive. He thought he might have been in some state of shock.

There he was, enjoying his morning coffee, when in came Baxter to tell him that the Brittler family carriage had just pulled to a halt at the front steps. And a few moments later, Charlotte Brittler had burst into his parlor without so much as a preliminary 'hello.'

He sighed and closed the front doors. Quite the picture she had been too. Her cheeks always seemed to warm with a blush whenever she was in his presence. And her hair had been pulled back in a rush, so that as she spoke, small tendrils escaped her pins, framing her small, pale face.

He was losing track of where his plot ended and his affections began. He had to keep reminding himself that

Charlotte Brittler was a means to an end and that he wasn't really interested in her. Was he?

Surely it would be better for his life and future if he could develop some affection for the woman he had chosen to make his wife. But this was not some. She was distracting him. Every day that had passed since he'd last seen her had felt like a plague on his functionality. It wasn't right. He could hardly eat, and sleep was out of the question. Worry, guilt, and strain kept him up late into the night. He found peace in his work. In the steady, thoughtless, stroke of his brush on the canvas.

He sat down on the parlor room sofa that he had just vacated moments before, and stared morosely out at the rain. She was asking for the impossible. Not least, because he hadn't the foggiest idea how he would ever manage to pay her father back. Let alone to hand her complete and utter control of any future they might have. And if he did discover some way to pay back Thomas Brittler, what then? Mightn't he just accept the money he was owed and still refuse Logan's advances on his daughter? And what if she decided, after all, that she wasn't interested in keeping him? What then?

He couldn't leave that much up to chance. No. He had to act. Had to change his aim. Surely there were other girls that would come with enough wealth to keep Drexel Industries afloat? He could do a bit of digging and come up with a positive nest of them. What was stopping him? Nothing. Nothing, except that the thought of taking this sensible course of action caused his insides to churn with fury.

He'd chosen Charlotte. And Charlotte he would have. "But how?" he muttered aloud to himself. How could he do it?

At that moment, Baxter, the family butler, knocked softly on the frame of the still-open parlor room door.

"The post has arrived, sir. Shall I leave it here with you or take it into your workroom?"

"Here, please, Baxter," said Logan hurriedly. He uncrossed his legs and reached out a hand for the small bundle of letters.

He'd recently had the nasty impression that either his mother, his father, or one of their servants had been searching his work room. The space had begun to feel as though it had been violated in some way or another, although nothing was out of place. He was aware that this paranoia was as unhealthy as—or possibly even the result of— his lack of sleep, but he couldn't seem to shake the feeling.

He thumbed through the post. Three of the four letters were from debt collectors. They had URGENT stamped on the front of them in red ink. Logan frowned and laid these three aside. He'd have to find some way to appease them with the money he had received from the auction. Although it was merely a pittance compared to their ever-mounting dues.

The fourth was tucked inside an elegant, white envelope, and Logan picked it up curiously, examining the seal on the back. He flipped it over to search the return address for a clue as to who it could be from, but couldn't think of anyone he knew who would be writing to him from the Dakota Territory. Quite bemused, he reached for an ornately handled letter opener and slit it open.

Mr. Logan Drexel,

I have written to inform you that I have been called away in the course of my duties. A last-minute decision was made that required me to travel westward, and the length of my stay is still to be determined. This letter comes with an apology of sorts, as I realize that I will no longer be available on the 21st of March to discuss the future of our two companies.

I would refer you to one of my partners if I did not want to discuss this matter with you personally. So, knowing it will be of great inconvenience to you, I would like to invite you to join me here in the Dakota Territory for our meeting. I realize this will add many unanticipated costs to your journey, and Stanford Oil will be happy to cover the additional travel fees.

I'll be staying in Bismarck at the Harrison Inn. If you are agreeable, I would be delighted to meet you at your convenience. I cannot see a point in the near future that I will be returning to Ohio, so please send your answer by return of this address.

Most Sincerely,
Stephen Harkness

Logan let his hand drop, the letter just clinging to his fingertips. North Dakota? He wondered, grimly. He'd thought traveling to Ohio was exuberant. What on Earth was Stephen Harkness doing in North Dakota? It occurred to him that Stanford oil was expanding. Certainly, this could only be good news for Drexel Industries, as it meant that Harkness would possibly be more eager to take them on.

Logan sighed and reread the letter, then he laid it down on the table in front of him. It sat there, looking like one of the many seagulls that flocked to the harbor, caught in mid-flight. A fanciful thought came to him then—borne, no doubt, from the strain of his current predicament—wouldn't it be nice to fly away from it all? To escape from his father's mistakes and live the life that his grandfather had wanted for him?

If it had only been so easy, he would be with Charlotte now, not sneaking around and bribing footmen to let him sing drunkenly at her window. He wouldn't be painting her smooth skin in the silence of the night, he'd be touching it.

He'd have been the chairman by now, making honest decisions for the benefit of the company, but instead, he'd been taught to lie and cheat. He'd aided his father in their downfall. He might as well have been the one pulling the strings, so deep was his betrayal.

He sighed again and pressed a palm to his forehead, trying to ease the ache that rarely vanished from the point between his eyebrows.

He had nothing. Absolutely nothing to offer the people who had the capability to make or break him. Nothing to lose.

His head snapped up so fast that he cricked his neck. Rubbing it, he continued to think. There it was. A simple fact. He had nothing to lose, and everything to gain.

Logan flipped over Stephen Harkness' letter and reached blindly for a pen. He was always able to think better on paper.

When everything came down to a point, Logan had one goal, and that was to create a successful merger in order to salvage what was left of his grandfather's company and the family's dignity. He scribbled down Stephen Harkness' name.

He needed money and a good amount of it. He needed to be able to show Harkness all that Stanford Oil had to gain by taking them on. He had to give the appearance that Drexel Industries' profit margins were high, because unless he received some sort of payout soon, the company and his family's entire reputation would go up in flames. And if that happened, his father would go to prison, and likely Logan alongside him. He needed help.

Charlotte's determined face flashed before his eyes, and he scribbled down her name too. Charlotte. Like it or not, he needed her. It had been about her money in the beginning, but that had been before she had taken hold of him. He would marry her now even if she were as broke as he was; her current status of wealth was, however, rather important. He put a dollar sign beneath her name.

Now, to get to Charlotte, Logan needed her father's approval. He scribbled down Thomas Brittler's name beneath his daughter's. And to get to Thomas Brittler, he needed a plan.

Logan sat back on the settee and tapped his pen on his knee, thinking hard. Charlotte's idea had merit. Most men, apart from his father, appreciated honesty and a willingness to admit one's mistakes. But if Logan were to go to Thomas Brittler in the strictest confidence—a man he did not know and had no reason to trust—what was to stop him from turning Logan and his father over to the authorities? He would be taking an enormous risk.

Logan stood and began pacing around the room. He feared the entire house would soon have a worn path around the carpets and floor.

Thomas Brittler was a business man. Surely he would see the advantage of Logan offering to return his stolen money. But then again was the problem that Logan had no way of managing this. He had no possible means of returning Thomas Brittler's funds to him.

A low, slinking thought crept into his mind then, rather like a snake winding its way out from long grass. Thomas Brittler had no proof. If he had, he never would have sat by and allowed Logan's father to get away with the deed. He'd have reported him long ago. And if he had no proof, there was no way he had any knowledge of the Drexel's coming failure. According to the world, the partners, even the workers, Drexel Industries was flourishing.

The profits that were made from the factories were being turned right around and poured back into them to pay wages, and salaries; to buy materials and make repairs. What little that was left was scrounged up by his father and tossed to the wind. Logan would have had little to no control if it hadn't been for a tiny clause in his grandfather's will that insisted that Logan took control of the payroll once he'd turned eighteen. There had been several arguments on the subject, several attempts by his father to take hold of the responsibilities and to keep Logan from it, but to no avail.

His grandfather had wanted Logan to have the responsibility of others livelihoods under his fingers from a young age. He'd wanted him taught what it felt like to have to care for someone other than himself. And he'd been right to do so.

Logan glanced, for the first time in a very long time, at the photograph of his grandfather hanging on the wall next to the bookcase. He tried not to look at it very often. The old man's eyes always fell on him with imagined resentment. Logan often wondered if his grandfather did not look down on him and shake his head sadly.

"I'm trying," he told the portrait. He moved across the room to it. He looked more like his grandfather than his father ever had. They had the same stubborn chin, and the same wiry, bristling beard. "I'm trying my best. I don't want to do this, but I can't see any other way."

He spoke of the merger he had been planning with Stanford Oil. If he could pull it off, the family, the workers, the company, it would all be saved, but the price was great.

Stanford Oil would take full control of Drexel Industries. The company, and its past—founder and all—would be virtually swallowed by their competitor.

Logan sighed and shook his head, looking away from the portrait's accusing stare. "I just don't see another way," he whispered again. He went back to the hastily scribbled notes on the coffee table.

He would go to Thomas Brittler. He would tell the man the truth and he would offer to return the stolen money, but he would be very careful about telling Thomas Brittler when he would have it. If the merger was a success, Logan would be sure to take a portion of the payout and hand it back to Thomas. If it was a failure... Well, he'd just have to cross that bridge when he came to it.

Thomas took up his pen and drew several arrows connecting the three names there. He needed Thomas Brittler's money to make a good impression on Stephen Harkness. He needed Charlotte so that he could get to her father's money. And he needed Stanford Oil to merge with Drexel Industries to salvage his grandfather's company. When that happened, he could give back the money his father had stolen from Thomas Brittler. If it didn't—Logan sat down his pen and folded up the letter, tucking it into his coat pocket—he couldn't think like that. This was going to work. It *had* to work.

Chapter Ten

Logan made his way along the high street with his mind whirring frantically. The cruel February wind yanked at his fine woolen coat, and he kept his shoulders hunched against the onslaught of rain. There hadn't been a cloud in the sky when he'd set off from Drexel Manor an hour ago, but now, as he neared Thomas Brittler's office building, clouds had rolled in and the sky had split open and vomited upon his head.

It'd been foolish of him to walk, but he'd thought the activity might clear his mind. It hadn't. He approached Brittler Steel with rain leaking down his collar and soaking into his shirt. His hair, finally devoid of a hat after weeks of covering up the healing mark Charlotte's vase had left, was dripping wetly into his eyes and beard. Catching sight of himself in a shopfront window as he passed, Logan growled irritably. Nice. Very professional, he thought in fury, and he proceeded down the next block to the corner of 4th and Main.

Thomas Brittler's office was a large, two-story building with several windows decorating the upper floor, and Brittler Steel and Co. written on a swinging sign over the entrance.

Logan shook off his coat and made an effort to wipe the dripping hair from his eyes before he mounted the small set of stairs and pulled open the door. The interior was spacious, and thankfully, very warm. A wood fireplace sat in the corner of the room behind a heavy desk.

The man sitting behind the desk was young and bespectacled.

"Logan Drexel to see Mr. Brittler," he said solemnly as he approached. The young man's eyes skated down the hem of Logan's coat to the small puddle he was creating on the carpet beneath his feet.

"Would you like a towel?" he whispered conspiratorially, "before I let him know you're here?"

Logan's shoulders relaxed. "Yes, please," he said in relief.

The desk clerk jogged out of sight and returned a moment later with a soft, fluffy towel in his hand. "You chose a lousy day for a stroll, sir," he said with a smile.

"You're not wrong," growled Logan. "Thank you." He accepted the towel with a nod and glanced at the clock just behind the desk. He was still a few minutes early.

He took off his coat and tried to straighten his hair once more. It fell limply into his eyes, causing him to let out another growl of frustration.

"I have some pomade in the drawer here," said the clerk. He slid a small tin can across the counter to Logan.

"You're rather prepared."

"A good first impression can work wonders where Mr. Brittler is concerned," said the clerk.

Logan snorted. "I think I've rather wasted that chance already," he muttered, but he shrugged and dipped his fingers into the tin with more thanks.

A few seconds later, Logan moved away from the mirror and faced the clerk with his arms held out.

"Better?" he asked.

"Much. I'll let him know you're here." The clerk smiled and disappeared up a large, winding staircase in the back of the room. Logan was left alone, standing foolishly beside the counter. He wasn't sure what sort of reception he could expect from Thomas Brittler. What did you say to the son of the man who stole your eldest daughter's inheritance?

He waited for at least fifteen minutes, and at last decided to take a seat on the edge of one of the spindly legged chairs near the front window. As soon as he'd sat down, the clerk reappeared.

"He's expecting you," he said with another friendly smile. Logan understood why they had placed this particular young man in charge of the front desk. He had a certain reassuring something about him, not to mention the fact that he'd bent over backward to aid Logan in lessening his resemblance to a drowned rodent.

Logan nodded and got to his feet.

"If you go up the stairs and walk along the hallway, his office is the last door on your left."

Logan nodded again and made his way over to the base of the stairs. Once there, he paused to consider what he was doing, and a granule of doubt slid out of his subconscious and surfaced. But then he pictured the amusement with which Charlotte had greeted their dangerous situation in the auction house. The way she had laughed as they escaped by the skin of their teeth.

The memory seemed to stiffen his resolve, and he ascended the staircase, his mind full of nothing but purpose.

The upper half of the office building was just as immaculately kept as the lower. The hallway was lined with the same ornate carpet, and the doors were trimmed in the same dark-stained wood.

Logan approached the last office on his left and knocked. There was a brief shuffling from within, and then he was bid to enter.

He turned the knob, and Thomas Brittler looked up from his desk with a grim expression of resignation on his face. He was a tall, thin man with a spectacularly bushy mustache. His arms were long, and his coat seemed to fit his shoulders a little loosely, as though he had recently lost a bit of weight due to strain.

"Mr. Drexel," he greeted Logan curtly, and he stood up to shake Logan's hand. His gaze was analytical, and very, very familiar. He had the same air about him that Charlotte had, the one that said that he would be a quite difficult person to please. Logan swallowed.

"Mr. Brittler. Thank you very much for seeing me today."

"What can I do for you?" Thomas asked, gesturing to one of the two armchairs in front of his desk.

Logan did not take the offered seat, but instead sat down his small briefcase and walked around behind it. He braced his hands on the back of the chair and took a deep breath.

"Sir, it has recently come to my attention that my family owes yours an apology of impossible proportions."

Thomas Brittler's eyebrows shot up into his hairline. Whatever he had been expecting, it wasn't that. He coughed.

"Is that so?"

"You see," Logan continued, approaching the desk and sinking down in the armchair directly opposite Thomas. He cleared his throat uncomfortably. "Forgive me," he said. "I don't believe that I have ever been so very uncomfortable in all of my life."

Thomas was frowning at him as though he couldn't quite believe his eyes.

"It has come to my attention, that through some complicated and underhanded means, my father managed to remove a vast sum of money from you and yours without your permission."

He couldn't look directly into Thomas Brittler's eyes as the sick feeling of shame crept into his gut once more. He spoke instead to the corner of the desk.

"I realize that your first instinct would be to report this theft to the proper authorities, but I ask," he swallowed again and forced himself to look into Charlotte's father's face. "I would like to ask you to give me the opportunity to return your money to you, so that my family and yours might avoid any potential scandal."

To his dismay, Thomas's face darkened with fury at these words. "How long have you known?" he asked quietly. He was glaring at Logan with undisguised ferocity.

Logan sat back in his armchair. "I'm not sure, exactly," he said matter-of-factly, crossing his left ankle over his right knee and rubbing his thumb and forefinger over his temples. "I had an inkling that he had done something of this sort, but I recently heard, through a source that I'd rather not disclose, that you suspected him as well."

If Logan had thought that Thomas had looked furious before, he had been wrong. The look on the man's face was murderous. "Do you not realize what this deception has cost us?!" he shouted, slamming his fist down on the desktop. "My daughter's inheritance was stolen out of her very hands the moment she came of age. Before she ever even had a chance to lay a finger on the money. I could do nothing for her! Nothing!" He looked quite as though he would like to seize Logan around the throat and throttle him.

"I'm so sorry, sir. I... could do nothing to prevent my father's actions."

"You could have turned him in yourself!"

"And watched my grandfather's company crumble under the onslaught of deliberations that would drain every resource we had left!" Logan was surprised to hear the vehemence with which he defended his own choices. "I've made this decision. I've come to you first. I want to make this right."

Thomas Brittler stood up. He began to pace.

"I have no right to ask this of you," Logan whispered, with a feeble shrug. "But I've no choice but to deal with this quietly. I am offering to return every cent you lost. Even if you were to turn my father in yourself, your money would be caught up in litigation so long that you'd lose at least half of what was stolen anyway. And to add insult to injury, you've no proof."

Thomas stopped his pacing, and his gaze fixed on Logan as though he were attempting to see through his skin and determine the color of his soul.

"Why?"

"Why what?" asked Logan. He felt exhausted. He needed sleep.

"Why are you attempting to return the money now? Dianna's inheritance was lost to us more than eight years ago. Why now? What do you have to gain?"

Logan sighed. He deliberated for a moment. Then, finally, he decided that the truth was his best option.

"I think you know my reasons," he said in a defeated voice.

Silence rang through the office as though Logan had fired a gun.

"No," said Thomas. "No, I think I would like to hear you explain them."

Logan sighed again and climbed to his feet. His head spun, and he tried his best not to sound as worn as he felt. "Sir, I'm afraid I have found myself quite enamored by your daughter, Charlotte."

Thomas turned abruptly away from him, and his eyes fixated on the dismal gray rain that still pattered against the office windows.

"I'm afraid she is quite interested in you as well," he said after a moment. His shoulders rose and fell quickly with his breath, and Logan held his own, waiting. Waiting, and then Thomas said: "I appreciate your honesty, but I cannot allow you to court her."

Logan felt the blood drain from his face as Thomas Brittler turned to look at him once more. He nodded, not trusting himself to speak.

"Still," said Thomas as he stalked back across the room to sink down behind his desk once more. "I am not unreasonable. If you can prove to me that your intentions are honorable, and that I may hold you to your word, I may consider it."

Logan felt his face break into his first smile in days. "There is a chance, then?"

"I have never been one for absolutes," said Thomas, but he did not return Logan's smile. "But, I do not want to give you false hope."

"What can I do, sir?"

Thomas leaned back in his chair, his anger had gone as quickly as it had come. It was clear that, like Charlotte, Thomas's temper sparked and then was immediately smothered. He looked intrigued.

"I will not pretend that I am delighted by your proclamation, but I find myself rather impressed at your courage. I'll give the matter some thought. In the meantime, I'll have my solicitors draw up a contract for the return of the funds."

Logan nodded. "I have a payment of sorts with me today," he said. "I brought cash. I wanted to give you a demonstration of my good will." He reached into his briefcase and unearthed the money from the auction of his painting.

He'd finished three more since Charlotte had come to visit him, and he was now speaking with the keeper of the auction house about holding a private gallery.

Thomas's eyes widened at the sight of the bills.

"If it would be agreeable to you," he said hesitantly, "I would like to make the payment in several separate installments for the time being, with the full amount coming by the beginning of Spring."

CHAPTER ELEVEN

Charlotte had been on edge for weeks, waiting for the smallest hint from her father; waiting to hear whether Logan had found a way to reach him. There hadn't been a whisper, not from either of them. Although father's solicitors were visiting the house more often than was usual, apart from that, everything seemed normal. And that made Charlotte very nervous. Perhaps she had misinterpreted Logan's feelings? Perhaps he wasn't as interested in her as she thought? Perhaps he'd given up on her altogether and moved on to more available fare?

She didn't know why, but every time this thought occurred to her, Charlotte invariably moved outdoors in search of fresher air. Ever since she'd first seen Logan Drexel, she'd felt a claim, as though he belonged to her, whether he liked it or not, and she couldn't seem to dislodge the feeling. It was like an irksome parasite was gnawing at her insides. She loathed the man, and yet she longed for him. Logan Drexel, apart from being very handsome, added a certain amount of excitement to her life that she had never known existed.

It was late on Thursday afternoon, and Charlotte was sitting at the large grand piano in the music room with an elbow propped up on the keys, staring out of the window. Rays of sunlight fell through the glass, illuminating the dark circles beneath her bright green eyes. Her mind had traveled the streets of Manhattan and skated over the highest rooftops in search of peace, but to no avail. She'd not sought another one to one meeting with Logan Drexel since her extraordinary proclamation in his sitting room, and as the days slipped by, she felt as though a bit of herself was slipping away with them.

The clock on the mantle chimed two, and Charlotte looked around as the door to the music room creaked open.

Accompanied by a flurry of bustling skirts and taffeta, Samantha Brittler entered the room, looking extremely excited.

"Charlotte," she said, moving forward to sit on the piano bench beside her daughter. "There's been a development."

Charlotte couldn't muster up the energy even to feign interest. She gazed at her mother in the same unperturbed manner that she had been contemplating the window. Samantha was smiling eagerly. "Look," she whispered, "Look at what I have in my hand."

Charlotte glanced down obediently and saw nothing more than one of her mother's customary dinner invitations. It was a fussy little thing, adorned with a small, satin blue ribbon. Charlotte always liked to imagine the expression on the recipient's face when they received it.

"Are we having a dinner party?" she asked in a bored voice. "Next to which eligible bachelor am I required to sit?"

Samantha's grin merely broadened and she whacked Charlotte's hands playfully with the sealed envelope. Charlotte had never seen her looking so delighted.

"I'm inviting Logan Drexel," she all but squeaked.

And now Charlotte smiled. That was all it took. His name. And she suddenly felt lighter than air. "How did you manage to convince him?" she asked her mother, taking the little cream envelope from her and gazing at the address on the front. She spoke of her father. The last thing she had heard on the subject had been that Logan Drexel was about as welcome in their house as dry rot.

"I didn't," said her mother. "I'm not sure what made him change his mind, but apparently, Mr. Drexel has been visiting him quite regularly at his office in town."

"Really?" asked Charlotte. She was elated. So, Logan hadn't forgotten about her after all.

"Yes! I overheard your father talking to his solicitor about some sort of payments Logan has been making to the company. And I thought, 'well, it doesn't sound as though he's adverse to doing business with the Drexel's.' So, I took a chance, and I asked him, and he said he thought it would be alright."

"Well," said Charlotte, standing up and moving around the grand piano to hide the sneaking smile that had slunk over her face. "I didn't expect that."

"Nor did I! But how wonderful! I really thought he was a charmer, that one. And you were so taken with him."

Charlotte huffed. "What makes you say that?" she asked evasively.

"Charlotte Brittler, I would beg you not to insult my intelligence. You were clearly enthralled with the boy. I've never seen you so dreadfully mopey since the day you were born."

Charlotte shook her head, feeling as though she were sinking into a pool of thick, dark mud. "He's much too..."

"Too what? Handsome? Wealthy? Well connected?"

"Mother," interrupted Charlotte with a grimace. "Those are things you would like to see in one of your daughter's prospective suitors."

Samantha Brittler smiled in satisfaction.

"I'll be inviting the Cases and the Hanson boys as well, I think that will provide plenty of entertainment for the evening?"

"I suppose so," said Charlotte. She smiled at her mother, who couldn't have looked more pleased if she'd just been crowned queen of England.

"Go get your sisters. Let's go into town."

"What for?"

"I want you all to have new dresses for next Saturday night."

Charlotte rolled her eyes and went to do as she was told. As she exited the music room she glanced back at her mother. "Thank you, Mama," she said quietly.

Samantha Brittler looked up. "What for, dear?"

Charlotte smiled. "For being on my side."

The following week slid by more slowly than any other Charlotte could ever remember. When Saturday came at last, she had to exercise a lot of restraint not to openly display her excitement. She was particularly eager to avoid fueling her family's suspicions about her affection for Logan, especially where her father was concerned.

It was clear to her, however, that her plan must have worked. Logan Drexel had, in the space of a few weeks, gone from being a name never mentioned beneath the Brittler's roof to being invited to join them for a formal dinner. Charlotte couldn't imagine how he had managed this feat with his family's current financial situation, and she wasn't sure if she even wanted to know.

Saturday morning dawned, bright and cheerful. It was the first really fine day they had had in a good long while. The Brittler's took their breakfast together on the back porch, all except their mother, who often breakfasted in her room. Noelle was all smiles and suspicious glances. Sarah-Jane was lost in her own world, and their father was reading the paper with the air of one avoiding something unpleasant. There was no mention of the dinner party that morning. In fact, the Brittler sisters were all rather quiet. Charlotte sipped her tea and tried her best not to let her elation show on her face. After their very quiet breakfast, the sisters moved into the upstairs library in the back of the house.

"What time are they supposed to be here, again?" Noelle asked for the umpteenth time that afternoon. She was staring out the side window, into the yard, as though she expected to catch sight of their guests coming up the drive.

"Would you please relax, Elle," grumbled Sarah-Jane. She looked up from the book in her lap. It was an old, dog-eared copy of The Lady of the Lake. "What are you so excited about? I never had the impression that you cherished an interest in either of the Hanson boys and the Cases' daughter, Eleanor, has always seemed rather dowdy to me."

"You could be a bit nicer, Sarah-Jane," muttered Noelle reprovingly. "It's been a good long while since we've hosted any sort of party at all. And mother sent a note to Mr. Williamson this morning with an invitation."

Sarah slapped her book down onto her thighs. "How can she have forgotten to invite him in the first place? I just..." she sighed and glared over at Charlotte. "I know she's excited about Logan Drexel, but that's no reason to dismiss everyone else."

"She hasn't dismissed Mr. Williamson. She just had a momentary lapse. She likes him very much. You know she does," said Charlotte.

"Hummph." Sarah pushed her reading glasses further up on her slender nose and shifted irritably in her chair before returning to her book.

In contrast with the rest of the week, Saturday afternoon sped away from her, and in what seemed like no time at all, each of the girls had retreated to her bedroom to change for dinner.

Her new dress was hanging, freshly pressed, from the wardrobe door. If truth be told, she was very happy with it. She'd spotted it on a mannequin in the dress shop window, showcasing a rather bold design of crimson and gold across the bodice and down the train. It had only taken a few minor tweaks before it fit her like a glove.

Penny moved into the room after a quiet knock. "How shall I do up your hair this evening, miss?"

"Oh... I think we'll leave it down tonight, Penny. Perhaps just a few curls?"

Charlotte wasn't sure what made her decide to leave her hair unbound. It wasn't exactly the most fashionable of decisions, but when she had slid on her dress and faced herself in the mirror, she was glad she had.

Penny tucked a few pins into the long tendrils around her face to keep them out of her eyes, and then she was ready.

"It's nearly four, Miss. Would you like to head down?"

"Yes, I think so."

The Brittler house was in rare form that night. As Charlotte descended the stairs, she thought the candlelight made the foyer look as though it were sparkling. She rounded the landing, intending to call out for her mother, and realized that there was someone standing beside the front door.

He looked as though he had been struck dumb by the sight of her, and Charlotte forgot to breathe. It was a few moments before she remembered how to speak.

"Mr. Drexel," she choked, trying and failing to smile. She moved down the staircase with as much grace as she could manage, now painfully aware of the stiff boning in her stays. "I'm so pleased you could join us this evening."

Logan seemed to have recovered himself. He took hold of her hand and bowed low over her fingers. Charlotte felt goosebumps rise up her arms in the wake of his touch, and she glared at him. Logan pretended not to notice. "My apologies, I didn't intend to arrive so early. Your butler let me in and bid me wait here a few moments."

Charlotte swallowed and wrested her fingers from his grip. "You remember our bargain?"

Logan looked surprised. "Was this the invitation of which you spoke?" he whispered. "Is this the official beginning of our courtship, then?"

"You know it is," hissed Charlotte, and she backed away from him, still quite unable to breathe. "And I would remind you of the stipulations that come into play in that eventuality."

"I didn't think that your rules would extend to casual greetings, Miss Brittler. You have my apologies once more. You may rest assured that I will remain perfectly well behaved from this point onward."

"Thank you." Charlotte smiled, feeling unaccountably nervous. "We can adjourn to the drawing room to await dinner." She indicated the open doorway to their left, and Logan gestured for her to lead the way.

The occupants of the room stood up as she and Logan crossed the threshold.

"Mr. Drexel," said Charlotte's father formally. He extended his hand, his eyes darting between them, as though he was trying to read their minds.

"I found him dawdling in the foyer," said Charlotte by way of explanation. Her mother was looking at her with something akin to pride.

"Well, I wouldn't call it dawdling," laughed Logan. He bowed over Samantha Brittler's hand and said, "Mrs. Brittler. What a pleasure it is to see your lovely face again."

Charlotte's mother blushed and patted her hair. "We're absolutely delighted to have you this evening, Mr. Drexel. Won't you sit down?"

Logan and Charlotte made for the same place on the settee at the same time and collided. Logan laughed, took hold of Charlotte's shoulders, and circled around her. Charlotte felt her cheeks flood with color. She glared at him again, and once more, he pretended not to notice. She glanced up to see both of her sisters grinning at her from the still-open doorway.

"My sisters," said Charlotte, recovering herself. "This is Noelle and Sarah-Jane."

"Good evening Mr. Drexel. Charlotte has told us so much about you," said Sarah, as she bobbed her head in a short curtsy.

Charlotte cleared her throat and cast Sarah-Jane a stern look. Sarah grinned wickedly.

Kincaid made his way into the room bearing a silver tray laden with glasses. He made no sign that he noticed anything out of ordinary in the present company, but as Logan accepted a small glass of port with thanks, Charlotte saw the acknowledgment that passed between them. She looked around, hoping no one else had noticed, but they were all engrossed in their own conversations.

Sarah and Noelle had taken seats on the opposite sides of the room.

Logan sat down on the settee beside her and sipped at his port, his eyes roving around the room.

"Your home is very beautiful," he said to Charlotte.

"It's nothing like yours," she responded, but she immediately wished she hadn't spoken. Logan's face darkened significantly, and he took a hasty sip.

"Tell me," said Logan, with what seemed like a great effort, "where is your eldest sister?"

Charlotte blushed again and glanced at her mother and father. "The last we heard, she was in Cheyenne,

Wyoming, but she said she wasn't going to be able to write very much."

"What is she doing there?" asked Logan, making no attempt to mask his curiosity.

"She-" Charlotte hesitated. They had never really told anyone where Dianna had gone. Their mother hadn't exactly forbidden them from mentioning it, but it was a tender matter. "She's married a ranch owner there."

"Oh?" Logan's dark eyes gazed intently into hers. It was as though her family was not present. "You disapprove?"

Charlotte smiled grimly and lifted her glass to her lips. "Not exactly." She said quietly. "In truth, I envy her a bit."

"Do you?"

"She's separate. She's gone off on her own. She's like Father. She wanted to make a life for herself with what she was given..."

Logan glanced at her parents. Thomas Brittler was determinedly not looking in their direction, as though if he could avoid seeing Logan and Charlotte together, a courtship between them would be less likely to take place.

"What an interesting thought," he said. "I never would have taken one of the Brittler girls for an adventuress."

"No?" replied Charlotte, quirking her brow.

"Not until recently." His whisper was for her ears alone, and it made Charlotte shiver.

Kincaid entered the room and everyone looked around at him. "Misters Abel and Rodger Hanson have arrived."

Two tall, broad-shouldered young men entered the room with identical smiles of enthusiasm.

"Mister and Misses Brittler," said Rodger, stepping forward to wring the hands of each of his hosts. "Thank you so much for inviting us here tonight."

"But of course, boys!" boomed Thomas. He was fond of the Hansen brothers. Charlotte rather thought that both of her parents were hoping one of the boys might catch Noelle's wandering eye. They seemed to be fighting a losing battle, in Charlotte's opinion.

Noelle greeted each man cordially enough, but it could not have been plainer that she was not remotely interested in either of them. Sarah-Jane was darting excited glances at the parlor door every minute or so, eager for her beau to arrive.

Rodger and Abel shook hands with Logan, and Charlotte found herself caught in the middle of an immensely boring discussion about the game of polo. Apparently, Rodger and Abel were both involved in The Westchester Polo Club as well.

It came as a relief when the last of their guests arrived. "Mr. Williamson, Mister and Misses Case, and their daughter Eleanor," Kincaid announced.

A skinny, pallid girl entered the room behind her rather austere looking parents, and, upon catching sight of her, Logan choked on his port. Charlotte watched him, curious, as he swallowed heavily. "Excuse me," he coughed. Abel pounded him on the back.

Mr. Williamson swept into the room. He was a handsome man in the classic sense of the word. He was clean cut, clean shaven, and well-dressed, with dark eyes that matched the crisp bow tie around his neck. He grinned as he stepped into the room and swept them all a broad bow.

"So gracious of you to have me over once more," he said, beaming at her parents. "I daresay that you'll all tire of me before long."

"Oh, I doubt that," said Thomas, clapping Mr. Williamson on the shoulder as he approached. "How are you, Carson?"

"Very fine, very fine," he responded, and then his eyes found Sarah-Jane. It was an odd thing to watch. In that brief instant, as their eyes locked, Charlotte would have said that Carson's features melted a bit. His gaze softened, his jaw relaxed, and as Sarah danced forward to greet him, she seemed to glow a little brighter than the rest of them.

Charlotte didn't know what to make of it. A moment later, she was distracted once more. Eleanor Case seemed to be undergoing some sort of mental strain. Her jaw had tightened, and a muscle had begun to twitch in her cheek. She glanced at each of her parents, who were both looking rather startled.

"Err... is everything alright, Gregory?" Thomas asked Mr. Case. He had just noticed the expression on his friend's face.

This question drew the eyes of everyone in the room to the scene unfolding before them.

Mr. Case cleared his throat, still staring at Logan. "I didn't realize you and Mr. Drexel were acquainted," he said quietly.

Thomas raised his eyebrow.

Logan, it seemed, had found his voice. "Mr. Case, it is an honor to find myself in your family's presence once more."

Mr. Case was tugging at the collar of his shirt, and as Logan spoke, there was no disguising the look of fury that slid onto his face. He took a measured step in Logan's direction and, to everyone's surprise, he held out his hand.

Logan appeared just as taken aback as everyone else but accepted the handshake with a hesitant smile. Mr. Case's responding grin was an ugly thing, and Logan suddenly winced. It looked to Charlotte as though Mr. Case was trying to squash Logan's fingers together. His knuckles were white.

As though on cue, the parlor door opened for a third time, and Mr. Grimsby slouched into the room, his bald pate gleaming. Mr. Case stepped away from Logan, his eyes never leaving his face.

"I hope you'll forgive my lateness," he puffed. A fine line of sweat was gleaming in his mustache. "My horse threw a shoe on my way here."

"You're just in time," said Samantha Brittler brightly. She glided forward as though on wheels, and Charlotte knew she was attempting to dispel the discomfort that had seeped into the room. "I'm sure they're just about to announce dinner."

It was a subdued group that made their way into the dining room. Charlotte was watching Logan, who did not seem to want to look at her. He was staring straight ahead, his expression gaunt. Mr. Grimsby was the chattiest of the lot. He shook hands all around and planted a wet kiss on the back of Charlotte's hand before they left the parlor. Now he was galumphing alongside her, dabbing at his face with a white handkerchief.

Charlotte sat herself down at her allotted place between Logan and Mr. Grimsby, now observing the expression on Eleanor's face, who'd been seated across from her. She was still pale, looked just as furious as her father, and appeared quite shaken. What was going on?

The first course was served, and Charlotte saw her father conversing in harsh whispers with Mr. Case. He looked mean, his face still full of that horrible forced smile. Charlotte couldn't stand it.

"What was that all about?" she whispered to Logan, under the pretext of arranging her napkin on her lap.

"I.." Logan looked as though he was trying not to move his lips. "I'm afraid we've crossed lines with another unfortunate victim of my father's."

"What?!" Charlotte overturned her goblet as Kincaid had made to fill it, and ice cold water seeped over the table cloth.

"I'm so sorry, Miss!" yelped Kincaid, but Charlotte waved him away.

"It's not a problem, Kincaid, honestly."

Charlotte reached for her goblet and righted it, avoiding eye contact with her mother, who was glaring daggers at her.

"How, pray-tell, has Mr. Case been wronged?" she hissed, doing her best to block Mr. Grimsby, who was leaning forward nosily, trying to catch each of her words in his oversized, puppy-dog ears.

"I'll explain later," growled Logan.

Charlotte sat up and took a deep breath, stowing her curiosity for another time. Then she directed her next question across the table at Eleanor. "Eleanor, I'm so glad you all made it out this evening. How have you been fairing? Are you still sketching?"

Eleanor's wintry expression was hastily modified into one of polite interest. "Oh yes. Mother and I spent the day in Central Park a few weeks ago. It was quite the perfect day for it."

"I hope you brought them along?"

"They're in the carriage."

"How wonderful! I can't wait to see them."

"Speaking of art," said Eleanor. "Have you seen any of those pieces? The new ones that everyone keeps talking about?"

"Oh yes," said Mr. Grimsby. "I purchased one at the auction only a few weeks ago."

"Did you really?" said Eleanor excitedly. "I'd love to have one. Do you have any idea who it might be that paints them?"

"No, not a clue," said Mr. Grimsby, patting his lips with a napkin. "I must say, though, they are fabulous pieces. If I could have every single one that he does, I would. But I can't seem to get my hands on them fast enough."

"Do you like them, Charlotte?" It was Logan. He looked quite curious.

"I've only seen the one," she admitted, picking at her food. The talk petered out.

Charlotte felt that she might soon collapse under the strain. Her smile was a little too broad, she could feel it shivering on her face. Her muscles were starting to stiffen. She made a concentrated effort to relax and then turned to Mr. Grimsby.

"How are you dear, Mr. Grimsby. I hope your mother's health is gaining?"

There. That should keep them occupied for a moment. It was much easier to listen to Mr. Grimsby wailing on about his mother's failing stamina—as far as Charlotte knew, the woman had never suffered from anything more than the common cold—than to try and force conversation. She let her thoughts wander, making the occasional moan of pity that was required, and all the while keeping an eye on her father and Mr. Case at the other end of the table.

By the looks of things, her father's tremulous, hard-won approval of Logan Drexel was about to disappear between the floorboards. Despite what he may or may not have done in the past, Charlotte was determined not to let that happen. Her mind grappled with possibilities, but nothing in the nature of a brainwave occurred to her.

The second course arrived and the conversation continued haltingly between bites. Logan was very quiet. She hoped he was thinking of a way out of this abhorrent situation because she had drawn a blank.

It was during the third course that it happened. Mrs. Case, who until that moment had been babbling ceaselessly next to Abel Hanson, suddenly clutched at her throat. Charlotte scrutinized her as the woman made a horrible retching noise.

"Mrs. Case?!" came her mother's shrill voice. A ripple of alarm went around the room, and Logan stood up so suddenly that his chair toppled over backward.

"Mrs. Case?!"

"Misses? What is it?"

As the room erupted, Logan leaped around the table and yanked Mrs. Case from her chair.

"What in the name of—!" Mr. Case blustered, having just noticed that something was amiss with his wife.

Before any of them could do more than yell with shock and outrage, Logan spun Mrs. Case around, planted his fist in her stomach, and began heaving her rhythmically into the air.

"Logan Drexel, unhand my wife at once!" shrieked Mr. Case, yanking at Logan's huge arms. It had absolutely no effect. Logan's grip was too strong. And a moment later, Mrs. Case gave a heave, a splutter, and a small chicken bone flew out of her mouth and skittered across the table in front of them.

The room was silent except for the woman's gasps. Logan slowly released her and lowered her into her seat with extreme care.

"Are you alright?" he asked, his hand on Mrs. Case's thin shoulder.

She nodded vigorously, still grasping her throat. She gulped, and then after a moment, she whispered: "Thank you."

Logan nodded too, and everyone settled back into their seats. Mr. Case knelt on the floor by his wife's feet, looking up into her face, which was devoid of blood. "Darling?"

"I'm fine, Gregory. I'm fine." She patted his hand. "I do think, though, that we may have to call it an early night." She glanced around the table, smiling with embarrassment.

"Of course."

Everyone stood up.

"Mister and Misses Case, you have my humblest apologies," whispered Mrs. Brittler. She came forward and reached for Mrs. Case's hand.

"Oh, my dear Mrs. Brittler, it was not your fault at all," said Mrs. Case, giving Samantha's hand a squeeze. "If anything, it was mine. I must learn to pay better attention when I'm eating." She shook her head, still looking rather ashamed.

"I'll have your carriage brought around at once," said Thomas Brittler.

He came back a few minutes later, and all three of the Cases made their way unsteadily out the door, Eleanor and Mr. Case supporting Mrs. Case in between them.

Charlotte danced nervously around the carriage door, trying her best to be of service while feeling quite as though she was merely in the way.

It was for this reason that she noticed her father tug Mr. Case to the side after his wife was safely situated, and she stepped behind the carriage so that she could listen without being spotted.

"Surely, Gregory, the man saved your wife's life tonight. The least you could do is give Mr. Drexel a word of appreciation."

"I refuse," Mr. Case whispered back. "One good act is not enough to redeem a man who has spent even a portion of his existence in such a depraved manner."

Charlotte heard her father sigh. "I'm sorry you see it that way."

"Be wary, Thomas. You may have already been deceived."

Charlotte glanced through the carriage window and watched her father nod. "I'm aware of his background, Gregory. But a man can change. I'd say we're both living proof of that fact."

It was Mr. Case's turn to sigh. He grasped her father's forearm. "Even if the exterior has been modified to fit its neighbor's, the bones of a house will remain the same," he said, sounding weary. "Thank you for the dinner. I'm sorry it was such a disaster. Rest assured that we will return the favor."

"No need to apologize," said her father. "I'll look forward to beating you at billiards."

They both laughed, and Charlotte beat a hasty escape around the side of the carriage. Eleanor was just clambering inside to sit beside her mother.

"Oh, Charlotte," she said. "There you are, I was hoping to have a word."

Eleanor glanced towards the Brittler's front door. The rest of the family and guests had gathered there, waiting for the Cases to depart.

"Be careful with Logan Drexel," she hissed, bringing her lips very close to Charlotte's ear. "He may not be all that he seems to be."

Charlotte glared at her. "You'll be pleased to know that I am perfectly aware of that fact."

Eleanor looked taken aback. "I only wanted to–."

"I quite understand, Eleanor. Thank you." She kissed the girl's cheek and then stepped back as Mr. Case climbed into the carriage. "I hope you feel alright tomorrow," Charlotte said to Mrs. Case.

"Oh, I'm sure I will recover," she said. Her voice was hoarse, but she smiled and waved as Mr. Case tapped on the roof, and the carriage moved off down the drive.

Charlotte shivered. The night had become bitingly cold once more.

"Why don't we go back in?" Logan's voice made her jump.

"I think I might take a walk around the garden," she said. "Kincaid?" she called a little louder. "Won't you bring me my coat?"

A few moments later Logan and Charlotte moved off into the enclosed garden in the Brittler's back yard.

"Explain," she demanded, not looking at him. She stomped along the path, trying to master her fear and confusion.

"Just wait a moment," said Logan, "and look at me, won't you?"

Charlotte had been avoiding his eyes. She didn't want to look up into Logan's handsome face and be disappointed. She was afraid that she might find out he'd been wearing a mask with her. That he wasn't truly interested in her at all, but only required her father's money. She knew this, though. She had entered into this agreement willingly. And he knew her conditions. She wouldn't marry without love.

Would he try and make her love him? Would he steal her heart from her only to break it in two? She hadn't thought of that. Surely, she would know. Surely, she would be able to keep herself safe.

But the confrontation with the Cases had brought something home to her. Eleanor was clearly heartbroken at the sight of Logan. What had he done to her? Had he used her up and then tossed her aside when she was no longer of any good? Would he do the same to Charlotte?

She faced him, mounting a defense.

Excitement. That was all she wanted out of life. That was all she had thought she had wanted from Logan. Excitement. Well, she'd gotten her wish. One night with him had been enough to prove that a life with Logan Drexel would be more than exciting.

"Why do the Cases despise you? What have you done?"

Logan's shoulders were hunched. He strode over to a lone bench against the bare hedges and sat down on it. "You know the kind of man my father is," he said. He was rubbing at the sides of his head. "He deceived many people. Myself included."

"Yes, but what did you do to them? What did you do to Eleanor?"

Logan flinched as though she had thrown a stone at him. "I'm afraid that I might have broken her heart."

Charlotte sighed. It was as she had suspected. "You used her. Did you promise to marry her?"

"No," said Logan, sitting up suddenly. "No. I wouldn't have done that."

"What happened?"

"I just... I might have egged her on a bit," he said grimly. "My father wanted me to make it appear as though a proposal was imminent so that he could talk her godfather into investing in some sort of imaginary scheme."

Charlotte sighed again. "She looked at you as though you had torn her heart straight from her chest," she said, sitting down on the cold bench beside him.

"I might as well have," said Logan. He leaned back on the bench and gazed at Charlotte, his eyes hard. "There have been others," he said. "Many others."

"How many?"

Logan shrugged. He looked mean. "Seven or eight. Maybe nine."

"Don't you care about them at all?"

"Don't look at me like that," growled Logan, he stood up and strode away from her. "You knew this," he barked. His voice had lost all sense of warmth. "You knew the things I'd done."

"I didn't realize—."

"That I'd done my father's bidding for years? That I'd bowed my head and watched him hurt people? Destroy families? I am worse than my father," he whispered. "What kind of man would aide in the destruction of everything and everyone around him? What kind of coward does that make me?"

Charlotte's eyes filled with tears. She didn't know what to say.

"I have never lifted a finger to stop him." Logan laughed. "I don't know why I chose this moment to try and make amends for the wrongs I have done. What hope is there for a man like me?"

"Don't say that," whispered Charlotte consolingly. She stood up as Logan turned away from her, and grasped his shoulder. "Forgiveness is always a possibility. You were so young."

"I wasn't," muttered Logan. "I was old enough to know better. I knew, somewhere inside me, I knew what he wanted me to do was wrong. Else why would I try to end it?"

"Exactly," said Charlotte with a smile. "And that makes you very, very different from your father."

Logan looked at her, and some of the anger and self-revulsion drained from his face. He glanced down at her hand, still clasping his arm, and his shoulders slumped. "I won't bother you anymore," he said.

"What are you talking about?"

Logan raised an eyebrow. "I rather assumed that you'd be searching for a way to dispel my interest. This is the end of things between us, isn't it?" He peered at her.

"Let's not be too hasty, Mr. Drexel," said Charlotte, matter-of-factly.

She relinquished his arm and stepped away from him, and a broad grin spread across his lips.

"You don't want to end things?"

"Before they've even begun?" asked Charlotte, sarcasm bellying her tone. "Why on Earth would I want to do that?"

Chapter Twelve

The squeak of the garden gate and a characteristic huffing and puffing announced the arrival of Mr. Grimsby in their midst. Logan felt a sudden stab of annoyance. What was this man doing? He tailed after Charlotte like a love-sick puppy after its master.

"Ah, Mister Drexel, Miss Brittler. Would you care to join us for a game of cards? The cook has brought up a tray of snacks for anyone who didn't eat enough at dinner. Miss Brittler, you should have something, you look dead on your feet."

Charlotte looked rather affronted. "We'll be in in just a moment, Mr. Grimsby, thank you."

Logan waited for the man to turn and head back inside, but he did not. He stood waiting for them, his bulbous chest heaving with the amount of exertion it had taken him to walk to the garden. The poor fellow did seem quite out of sorts. "Mr. Drexel, I took the liberty of bringing your coat out for you. I thought perhaps you might be chilled."

Logan raised an eyebrow at the man. "That was very kind of you, sir," he said, doing his best not to let his annoyance show on his face. He and Charlotte exchanged a look, and then, together, they moved toward the garden gate.

"For what it's worth," Logan whispered, leaning forward to breathe in Charlotte's ear. "I think you look lovely." He carefully avoided brushing her arm as they walked back inside the house, determined not to give her cause for second thoughts.

All the rest of the night, Mr. Grimsby's presence began to grate more and more on his nerves. He liked Charlotte to sit next to him at the game table and hung onto her every word as if it was his lifeline. Charlotte appeared not to notice the older man's obvious infatuation with her. She laughed and touched his arm casually, as though they were the best of chums, but Logan couldn't help but notice the way Mr. Grimsby was watching Charlotte. Possessively. Wantonly. It made Logan's skin crawl.

Little by little, the evening began to wind down. Logan wasn't stupid. He'd noticed Mr. Case and Mr. Brittler speaking intently at the dinner table before Mrs. Case's unfortunate scene. He could feel Thomas Brittler's eyes upon him and knew that he was being judged by his every move. He'd never been watched so closely in all his life, and the thought made him nervous, and a bit clumsy.

Finally, it was time for him to take his leave. Charlotte walked him to the front door.

"Well," said Logan, sliding his arms into his overcoat, "I can't say it wasn't an interesting night."

"It was rather eventful," muttered Charlotte. She was rubbing her bare arms. It was colder here by the door. Logan lifted his hand as though he was going to pull her to him, but thought better of it. He excused the gesture by reaching for his hat, but her smirk told him that Charlotte had not missed the twitch of his hand. He grimaced at her, and she laughed.

She was truly a marvelous creature. Her red hair glimmered in the dim light, and her laugh made him feel as though he had just taken a sip of warm, cinnamon whiskey. He couldn't help it. He grinned too.

"Do you think your father was pleased with my performance?" Logan asked, his voice joking. "I'm not sure I came up to scratch."

"You saved Mrs. Case's life tonight, Logan," Charlotte reminded him. She shook her head. "If I know Father, he's going to want to keep you under his nose for a good long while before he decides to pass judgment on you. But know... he was pleased. He also seemed rather impressed with your quick thinking. If you hadn't been here, Mrs. Case might have choked to death at our dining room table. Where did you learn to do that?"

"Oh, it was just something I picked up," said Logan with a roguish wink. He bent forward with his hat in his hand, and swept Charlotte a low bow. "Until next time," he whispered.

With that, he stepped out into the cold night, shutting the front door behind him.

Emboldened by his success at the Brittler's the previous night, Logan saddled his horse, hitched a small cart up behind it, and made his way into town early the next day. The keeper of the auction house was pleased to see him.

"Mr. Drexel," he said cheerfully, coming right up to Logan and wringing his hand. "You'll be pleased to know that-."

"Shhh," pleaded Logan, looking around at the crowd of people milling about in the entrance hall.

The auctioneer's mustache bristled. "Yes, of course," he said embarrassedly. He glanced around and then led Logan into his private office.

Logan shut the door behind himself and turned to face him.

The auctioneer was a short, barrel-chested man with a very thick neck. "You'll be pleased to hear that I've had many offers on your work and accepted the highest two."

"Wonderful," said Logan, clapping his hands together. "That's absolutely fantastic. I've brought you six more pieces."

"Six!" exclaimed the auctioneer, practically dancing on the spot. "Six more? You do work fast, Mr. Drexel."

"Is that enough for you to host a gallery display?"

"Certainly! I'll plan a large unveiling for next month. The buyers will be thrilled. Oh, I wish that you'd let me tell them who you are."

"No," said Logan firmly. "The high society of New York glories in the mysterious. If you tell them who I am, it'll take all the fun out of their coming. I guarantee it."

The auctioneer looked doubtful, but he brightened quickly. "I'll have my assistant bring your cart around the back so that they don't see us bringing them in," he said.

Logan left the auction house feeling, for the first time, as though things might actually work out the way he had hoped. His paintings were selling well, not well enough to supplement the actual fortune that Drexel Industries should be worth, but well enough for him to start paying off some of the company's many debts.

He was setting aside one thousand dollars each week for Thomas Brittler. A large amount to some, but in reality, it was very little compared to what his father had stolen from the Brittler family.

The afternoon found him sitting in his workshop. The canvas in front of him was blank. He stared at it. The more he painted her, the harder it was to conceal her identity. He knew that all of Manhattan was seething with curiosity about the unknown painter's obsession with the red-haired beauty. His paintings were selling better than he had ever hoped, and the more he brought to the auction house, the happier the auctioneer was. It was easing his mind to know that some of their massive debt was being siphoned away.

He was doing very well at keeping this from his father, though. As far as Berkley knew, the Drexel's were still sitting on rock bottom. Logan intended to keep it that way. The less his father suspected, the fewer inquiries he would be making into the company's finances, and the less he would manage to throw away.

Logan hadn't spoken to his father since their last argument, and that was several weeks ago. They rarely passed each other in their vast home, as Berkley liked to keep different hours than his son. Logan had no idea where he went or what he was up to, and the feeling that it couldn't be anything good did not soothe his anxiety.

Logan exhaled violently and breathed in the smell of his musty, makeshift workshop. He'd taken an upstairs room, frequently used for storage, and brought in his easel. Little by little, it had expanded to include an old chest of drawers, a filing cabinet, and several paint-stained mugs of water.

The fireplace was full of a crackling fire, and seagulls circled outside the window. Condensation gathered in little droplets on the glass as the interior of the room fought back the chill of the outside.

Logan's thoughts returned, as they so often did these days, to Charlotte. Charlotte, and her laughing eyes, her mischievous smirk. Logan thought of how she had looked at the Brittler's dinner a few nights before. How she had comforted his guilt-driven mind as easily as she would have sung a babe to sleep. Then he was thinking of her holding a baby, and his thoughts were of marriage, and children and happiness. A happiness he did not deserve.

Children? thought Logan suddenly. He'd never wanted them before. He ran the end of his brush over the scruff of his chin as he contemplated a future with Charlotte, and then, smiling, he set his brush to the canvas.

The days did not warm as Springtime crept closer. As January drew to a close, Logan found himself making excuses to visit the Brittler house. Thomas Brittler watched him like a wrathful eagle, but he never made any attempt to dissuade him from coming. Mostly, Logan assumed, because Charlotte seemed to be enjoying herself just as much as he was.

"What about this one?" Logan asked her. He reached up as high as he could and pulled a book from the shelves in her father's upstairs library.

"Advances in the English Language 1875."

"How do you do that?" Logan growled, replacing the book and turning to frown at Charlotte.

"I've told you," she laughed, spinning her arms in a circle, and then flopped down onto the chair closest to the roaring fireplace. "I know every book in my father's library, and," she stood again, now glaring at him, "I know their place."

She bounded over to him, stretched onto her tiptoes—her body stretching beautifully—and moved the book he had just replaced to the correct spot. Her dress was palest pink today, and it flowed around her limbs in the most becoming of fashions. Logan was having difficulty keeping his eyes to himself, let alone his hands.

"That's ridiculous," he laughed.

"It's true," said Noelle through a yawn. She had dark circles under her eyes. "She reads more than a normal human ought to."

"You should talk," giggled Charlotte. "I saw your light on last night at four in the morning. You're not going to tell me you were working on your needlepoint."

Noelle blushed. "What were you doing out of your bed at four in the morning?"

"Just getting a drink of water."

"I'm sure," muttered Noelle. She cast a glance over her shoulder at Logan, who suddenly found himself intensely interested in an ugly bust standing on a plinth against the wall.

Charlotte and he had been out for a stroll in the moonlight late last night. He wasn't sure what had gotten into the prim and proper young lady he had met all those nights ago. She'd grown excitable, challenging, and playful ever since he had shattered that vase in the auction house. If he didn't know better, he'd think that he'd had a bad influence on her.

Last night had been particularly wonderful, and also, rather horrid. Charlotte had been unusually quiet as they made their way around the darkened streets of Manhattan.

"Are you scared?" he asked her.

"No," she said, much too quickly.

He smiled. "Would you like to hold onto my arm?"

Charlotte's shadowed face had turned toward him, and her hair danced around her cheeks, which were flushed in the darkness. He'd caught an image in his mind just then, and it was already transferring beautifully onto the canvas. The shadows would mask her identity, but he'd be able to fix this exquisite picture in his mind forever.

He'd never wanted to kiss a woman so much as he had in that moment. Her lips were pale in the darkness. He wanted to press his mouth to hers and bring back her color. Her vibrant, talkative, warmth. He needed to hold her in his arms, this brave, dangerous woman who had stolen his heart.

He moved towards her, and Charlotte seemed to recognize something in his eyes. She took a step back and came up against a brick wall. Logan still hadn't touched her. He didn't intend to break his word on purpose. He wanted her permission.

Slowly, without ever taking his eyes off her, Logan planted his palms on the wall, encasing her in his arms.

"Logan," she said warningly.

"I'm not touching you," he whispered.

She giggled. "Oh, is that the game we're playing?"

"What game?" chuckled Logan. He bent his head closer to her so that her sweet, warm scent filled his nostrils, and as he let out his breath, he watched her shiver.

"Logan," it was almost a whine.

"What?" he whispered in her ear, and he was delighted when she shivered again. "I'm not breaking any rules."

"You're too close."

"But, I'm still not touching you."

He could feel her warmth. She was seeping into his very bones, and he wanted her more than he had ever wanted anything in all his life.

Sarah-Jane entered the room just then, jerking Logan from his recollections. Everyone looked around at her. "Oh, hello, Mr. Drexel. I didn't know you were here," she said, smiling fondly at him. "Will you be joining us for dinner, again?"

"If your parents do not object."

Sarah rolled her eyes to the ceiling. "As if they ever would. Mother believes that you walk on the clouds with a harp and a halo in all of your free time."

All four of them laughed, but Logan privately hoped that Mrs. Brittler never found out just how wrong she was. He liked that someone thought of him as something other than the son of a thief.

He caught Charlotte's eye, and as they headed downstairs to the dining room, she gave him a small wink.

They moved as a group into the foyer, but as they turned to head for the dining room, a knock sounded on the front door.

"I'll take it! I'll take it!"

Mrs. Brittler came bustling into the room, looking extremely pleased about something. She waved away the butler and pulled open the front door.

"Mr. Jorge, at last!" she squeaked, clapping her hands together. "I've just cleared a place for it. Bring it this way."

A man in work grubs entered through the front door and nodded at the group assembled there. In his arms, he carried a carefully wrapped package about three feet tall and two feet wide. It looked oddly familiar to Logan, although he couldn't imagine why.

"Perfect, perfect. Bring it in here. I want to hang it in the drawing room."

"Mother?" asked Noelle interestedly, following after the workman. "What did you buy?"

"Oh, you'll see in a moment. You'll love it! It's the most fantastic piece."

Noelle, Charlotte, Sarah-Jane and Logan gathered against the far wall as Mrs. Brittler began directing the workman as though she were directing troops in battle.

"A little more to the left. Down a bit. Perfect. Let's see it uncovered."

Mr. Jorge reached up and untied a knot of string holding the package together. Piece by piece, the brown canvas cloth fell away and Logan choked.

He had painted Charlotte against a floral backdrop that looked, now that he thought about it, gratingly similar to the one she had sat on in his mother's parlor. He smiled as Charlotte looked at him.

"It looks like you," he said, grinning.

She slapped his arm. "It most certainly does not. You can't even see that woman's face."

"Is it by the same artist as the one at the auction last month?" asked Noelle, taking a step closer.

"The very same!" squealed Mrs. Brittler. She clapped again. "Isn't is gorgeous? I told the auctioneer to let me know if any more pieces came in. He sent me a note just yesterday!"

"I'd say this artist has an affinity for Scottish women, with all the red-haired portraits," said Sarah.

"Perhaps a particular Scottish woman," chuckled Charlotte. "It really is beautiful. It looks as though he's captured so much emotion. I don't understand how he can do it without showing her face. I do love it, though."

"Do you?" asked Logan. He was watching Charlotte's eyes darting over the canvas. His canvas. His work. And here was his muse before him.

"Oh yes, don't you?"

Logan grinned, his heart lighter than air. "I do."

CHAPTER THIRTEEN

It was midnight, and Charlotte was lying awake in her four-poster bed, staring out of the window. A shaft of moonlight fell across her face and illuminated her green eyes. She could just hear the sounds of Sarah-Jane's gentle snores echoing through the wall from the bedroom next to hers. The silence of the night held promise... and terror.

Charlotte Brittler was in love, something she hadn't quite expected. She had gone and fallen in love with Logan Drexel, and only she knew it for the complete and utter catastrophe that it was.

Today, her mother had taken her to pick out the lace for her wedding gown. A few days ago, she had overheard her father talking with Logan about finding them a place to live after they were married. Did they want to live here? Would they live in Drexel Manor, or would they find a place of their own?

A place of their own? It had never occurred to Charlotte that she would fall into the trap that she had foreseen. She didn't want to be another broken heart on Logan Drexel's list.

But he had proved out, hadn't he? He had charmed her parents. Made up for his past. Begged for forgiveness. He had been honest with her from the first, and she with him. She was very aware of the part her fortune played for him. When they married, they would have very little. Her inheritance would be used to pay off his father's debts, but her father oughtn't to know that, or he would never consider letting her wed him.

The fact that she was considering going through with it was proof enough to her. She loved Logan. She wanted to spend her life with him, but she had to be sure.

Charlotte Brittler was not a fool. She had worked so hard to separate herself from the situation. She'd wanted to observe Logan with an unbiased view, and get to know him without the drawback of girlish emotions misleading her every step. But they had led her, they had taken control of her and now there was no going back. Only forward. She was in love with Logan Drexel, and she was quite sure that he loved her as well, but she had to be certain.

For the third time in recent memory, Charlotte climbed silently out of her bed. She was going to see Logan. She had to know. Had to be sure. She would not enter a loveless marriage. She would not do it. She was going to find out how much he loved her.

It was very unlucky that the night was clear and the moon was full. Charlotte darted between patches of shadow and moonlight, determined not to be seen. She met Kincaid just outside the side door.

"Thank you," she whispered, and she took the reins in his hand and hoisted herself up onto her horse's back. "I'll be back before the dawn, don't worry."

"I'm still not sure that you should go alone, Miss."

"Don't fuss, Kincaid. I'll be perfectly alright."

"Be careful."

"I will be." Then she was off.

Once outside of the Drexel house, she couldn't hold back the fear. She rode her horse right up the front steps, raised her fist to knock, and then she stopped. The realization of what she was doing hit her. She lowered her hand.

It was the middle of the night. She couldn't just burst into Drexel manor and demand—the front door opened as she was turning away.

"Charlotte?"

"Oh, Logan. Thank the heavens above," she stepped inside the front door, pulling off her hood, and wringing her hands most convincingly.

"Charlotte, what are you doing here?" asked Logan. He was bleary-eyed and tousle-haired, and he had a smear of bright red paint across his right cheek.

Charlotte buried her face in her hands. She wasn't sure if she could manage to cry real tears, but she had to try.

"It's so dreadful, Logan. I'm afraid I shouldn't be here at all."

"When have you ever cared about that?" he chuckled, smirking.

Charlotte glared at him and stalked into the parlor. She was never very good at playing the lady in distress, and she had a feeling that Logan would see through her charade quickly if she tried to keep that up.

"What is it?" he asked, following her into the parlor and shutting the door behind them.

"It's—It's Father," she lied, avoiding Logan's eyes as he cocked his head to the side, trying to get a good look at her face.

"What's wrong with him? Is he ill? What's happened?"

"No, no. Nothing like that," she muttered hurriedly. The last thing that she needed was Logan to rush off to their house. "He's forbidden me to see you."

"He's what?!" yelled Logan. "I'm going over there right now. We'll sort this out."

Charlotte reached for him. "I'm afraid it's no good," she said, sadly, shaking her head. "He's said if you come near me again, he'll call the constable."

"What—why? Why would he do that? I was just there the other day! We talked for hours. He never said—." Logan was clearly panicking. "I can talk to him," he said and he made to head for the door again. "I'll make him see sense."

"It's no good!" cried Charlotte. "It's no good. Logan, if we want to marry, we'll have to do it without Father's blessing."

"What?! But I thought you—Just let me talk to him, Charlotte."

"You're not listening to me! I—I ran away, Logan. I ran out. He said if I went to you, he'd disinherit me. He'll do it, Logan. He knows I'm here."

Logan sank down onto the horridly floral settee. He looked drained. "What made him change his mind?"

"I don't know," whispered Charlotte. A powerful wave of guilt erupted inside her at the look on Logan's face. "He came home from the office today all of a dither. Told me I wasn't to be seeing you anymore. He said that he'd write you a letter and tell you to stay away. We argued a good long time... and then..."

Logan was looking defeated. His body had sunk into the sofa, his legs splayed weakly out to either side.

"That's it then?"

"That's it."

"Well, I suppose you better stay here for the night. I'll have Baxter make up one of the spare rooms. We can go to the courthouse tomorrow and register for our marriage license."

Charlotte didn't dare to hope. Did he mean what she thought he meant? "But what about my inheritance?"

Logan looked up at her as though she had spoken a foreign language. "Your inheritance?"

"What about the money?"

"Oh, my dear," Logan stood up, took two steps, and wrapped his arms around her. Finally. Finally. She breathed in the smell of him and sank into his warmth. His arms felt so good that she momentarily forgot what they were discussing. She inhaled deeply and then reached up and ran her fingers through his dark hair. "I'm sorry. I'm so sorry. What was I thinking? I would marry you if you were penniless. I would marry you tonight, now, in a heartbeat. But you're right. You must go back to your father. You must make amends. I cannot ask you to live a life of poverty with me."

"What?"

"You have to go home, Charlotte."

"No!" she cried. She pushed away from Logan, shaking her head violently from side to side. "No, I won't go."

"You don't know what you're talking about."

"I won't go, Logan. I won't leave you."

Logan sighed and took her hands in both of his. Gently, tenderly, he placed a kiss on the back of each, and then he smiled.

"Are you sure?"

Charlotte smiled back. "Logan Drexel, I have never been surer of anything in my entire life."

His eyes lit up. He looked like an overgrown school boy. "Wait here," he whispered. "Don't move. I'll be back in a moment."

Charlotte watched Logan fly out of the room, upending an end-table in his excitement, and then she heard the sound of his feet pounding away up the marble stairs.

A few moments later he returned, skittering into the parlor like so many scattered marbles. He stopped in front of Charlotte, straightened his shirt—which was hanging half-way out of his trousers—and bent down onto one knee.

Charlotte inhaled sharply. In his hand was a tiny, golden box.

"I meant to do it differently," he said, still grinning. "I had a whole day planned out, but if we're getting married tomorrow, this will have to do." He opened the box.

Inside was the most beautiful ring Charlotte had ever seen. A single, large diamond, surrounded by eight smaller ones, all set in a round circle, and inlaid with sparkling gold. It glittered in the single shaft of moonlight that slanted in from the parlor window.

"Miss Charlotte Brittler, will you do me the honor of-" he stopped as Charlotte burst into tears. Very noisy tears, not the pretty kind. She leapt away from Logan and gestured him up off his feet. "Wha- I..?"

"No, get up, get up!" Charlotte sobbed. "I've ruined it."

"Ruined what, darling? You haven't ruined anything!"

"Yes. Oh, yes, I have. Logan. I'm horrible. I'm a scoundrel. I'm a fool. I just love you so very much!"

"What is it? What's the matter?"

"Oh, Logan," Charlotte collapsed on the sofa in a heap, searching her pockets for a handkerchief. "I was such a fool. Can you forgive me?"

"Forgive what? Do you not want to marry me?"

"Oh no! Of course, I do!"

"Then what?" Logan was still on one knee, his hands outstretched, holding the ring. He looked positively baffled.

Charlotte cried harder than ever. "My father hasn't forbidden me to be with you. He never said anything of the sort."

"Then why lie?" asked Logan. He lowered his hands. "Why come here tonight at all?"

"I had to be sure." Charlotte's vision was blurred with her tears. "I had to know."

Logan sat back on his heels, his brow furrowed. Charlotte noticed that his feet were bare.

"You thought I wouldn't want to marry you," he said. "You thought I wouldn't want to marry you without the money."

Charlotte inhaled shakily, and then tremulously, she nodded.

Logan pursed his lips and stood. The ring box snapped closed in his palm. He was looking at her with an intense, calculating gaze. His eyes looked hard. Then he gave a sharp nod.

"Alright," he said. That was all. One word. Charlotte looked up at him, confused.

"Aren't you going to be angry with me?"

Logan smiled wryly. "Miss Brittler, if I were to be angry with you, I would be the worst sort of hypocrite. How could I be angry with you for doubting my intentions? I don't fault you. But..." he held up his finger as Charlotte opened her mouth to speak. "I do want to set a condition."

Charlotte's lips quirked up in the corner. She knew she must look a mess. She was an ugly crier. She'd seen Sarah-Jane shed pretty, glistening tears when she was upset. Charlotte's tears were hideous. She sniffed loudly, wiping her nose on the back of her sleeve and dabbing at her puffy cheeks.

"What sort of condition?"

Logan sank back down onto one knee and re-opened the golden ring box. Excitement lit inside Charlotte like the strike of a matchstick. "If you agree to be my wife," he said. "If you accept this ring, from the moment the band encircles your tiny, little finger, there will never be another lie between us."

The tears came again then. They flooded down her already swollen cheeks and pooled in the collar of her woolen coat. She nodded fervently.

"Then, Miss Charlotte Brittler," said Logan, a small catch in his voice, "will you do me the honor of becoming my wife?"

It was as though the match inside her had lit a fuse. A massive explosion took place in Charlotte's chest. She inhaled as Logan reached for her hand. He was looking at her in a way that made Charlotte feel ashamed for having ever doubted him. There was so much love in his expression. She'd never seen so much love on a person's face before.

"Mr. Logan Drexel," she hiccupped, "I will be your wife."

Logan leapt to his feet. With tears in his eyes, he fumbled with the ring box, wrested the ring from within, and slid it onto Charlotte's outstretched finger. His hands were shaking.

"I love you, Charlotte," he whispered. "I never believed I could love a woman so much in all my life. I will spend my entire existence making sure you are never, ever sorry that you said yes to me."

He bent down, wrapped his arms around her waist, and lifted her off the sofa. Charlotte squealed as Logan spun her in a circle, narrowly dodging the coffee table, and then they fell into a tangle of skirts and breathless giggles.

Chapter Fourteen

The day was rainy and depressing, but Logan felt as though he was carrying a talisman of sorts inside his chest. Something so wonderful and warm that even the dreary February weather couldn't take from him.

She had said yes. She had agreed to be his wife, and Logan felt very much like breaking into song as he skipped down the dirt path that led to the Brittler Family Estate. Feeling it might be a bit much, instead, he whistled cheerfully as he hopped up the front steps and knocked on the front door.

Through the rippled glass in the door, Logan watched the oblong shape of the Brittler's friendly and cordial butler, Mr. Hennesy, making his way to the front door.

"Hennsie! My dear fellow, won't you tell Mr. Brittler that I am here to see him?"

"Mr. Brittler?" said Mr. Hennesy doubtfully. "Wouldn't you like me to inform Miss Charlotte?"

"Oh no, shhh," he raised a finger to his lips. "Don't tell her that I'm here yet."

"Very well, sir," said Hennesy. If you'll follow me. Mr. Brittler is in the drawing room."

Humming, and with a jaunty skip in his step, Logan followed Mr. Hennesy into the house.

"Mr. Drexel to see you, sir," said Hennesy, and Logan stepped into the room. His expression fell as soon as he glimpsed the look on Thomas Brittler's face.

"I hope I haven't interrupt—."

"Get out." Mr. Brittler was pointing at the door with shaking fingers. "Get out of my house, boy."

Logan faltered. It was his nightmare come true. "Mr. Brittler?"

"You heard me," he said ferociously, jabbing his finger at the door again. "Get out. Don't you ever darken our doorstep again. Get out. Now, before I call the authorities."

"Mr. Brittler, if I could just have a moment, I'm sure we could..." Logan took a step back as Thomas advanced on him with his fist raised. He was clenching a white piece of parchment that had been folded over several times, and was now crumpled as he waved it furiously in Logan's face.

"I know what you are," he spat. "You're no better than your thief of a father," he threw the piece of paper down at Logan's feet. "Get out!" he screamed. "And if you ever come near my daughter again, you will be very sorry indeed."

Logan stooped to pick up the wrinkled parchment, a hollow pit developing in his stomach. "Mr. Brittler, I can explain this," he said, as he recognized it for what it was.

"I'll not listen to any more lies," hissed Thomas.

"This isn't what it appears to be."

"It's exactly what it appears to be!" Thomas was swelling with fury, his thin face was purpling. "You and your father are rotten to the core. Your entire family is in on this farce. You would do it, too. You'd take my daughter's money and run for the hills. You would have abandoned her!"

Logan looked down at the letter from Stephen Harkness, the one on the back of which, he had scribbled his thoughts and plan of action, and he understood. From this hastily drawn note, it looked very much like Logan intended to use Charlotte for her money, which, of course, he had. But that was then, in the beginning. Even as he had written this note, he had known he was falling in love with Charlotte Brittler. He had never meant it to look like this.

"Where did you get this?" asked Logan quietly.

Thomas was still glaring at him. The drawing room door opened and the rest of the Brittler household came in.

"What's all this?" demanded Charlotte. She looked absolutely terrified.

Mrs. Brittler looked just as scared as her daughter. Noelle looked confused, and Sarah-Jane appeared oddly satisfied.

"Show her," Thomas instructed, indicating Charlotte. "Show her what you have planned."

Logan shook his head. "This isn't at all what it seems," he whispered, but he held out the note to Charlotte, who read the letter on the front first.

"You're traveling?" she asked confusedly. "Father, why should it matter if he is traveling?" She flipped the letter over and gazed at the back. Her eyes widened, and Logan watched her swallow. She looked up at Logan, and he thought his heart would shatter.

"What is this?" she asked, a tremble in her voice now. "What does this mean?"

"It means," said Thomas, shaking with suppressed rage, "That your darling beau here intended to rob you blind after you were married."

"That's not true!" shouted Logan. "Charlotte! You know it isn't true."

She was still looking at him, and her eyes filled with tears. She crumpled up the letter in her fist and lobbed it into the fire, then she took a very deep breath, her chest heaving, and she came to stand beside Logan.

His heart gave a leap.

"Father, I am convinced that, no matter if his intentions were honest in the beginning or not, Mr. Drexel is being quite honest now."

Thomas Brittler's purple face stared between Logan and his daughter. "If you marry him," said Thomas, his chest still swollen, "he will destroy you."

Charlotte looked at Logan, and in her eyes—little though he knew he deserved it—he saw love, he saw compassion and understanding.

"I don't believe that he will," she whispered, and she reached for Logan's hand. He felt his grandmother's diamond engagement ring pressing into his palm. He looked down at their conjoined fingers and felt elated.

Thomas Brittler looked apoplectic. "You'll not get a cent," he said to the pair of them. "I won't allow it. You'll see, Charlotte. You'll see. The day will come that you regret this."

"I highly doubt that," she said. And, still holding Logan's fingers in her own, she pulled him from the room.

⚮

"How could you?!" a few hours later, Logan stood in his father's dusty, overcrowded office, gesticulating wildly at him. "What could you possibly have gained by sending that note to Charlotte's father? What good have you done?!"

Berkley Drexel observed his son with a look of utter incredulity on his face. "I'm afraid I don't have any idea what you're talking about," he laughed lightly, although it could not have been plainer that he wasn't at all amused.

"Oh, please," growled Logan. "Let's not play this game again. I'm sick of the lies. Out with it. I want to know why you did it."

"My son," said Berkley sarcastically, "if I had any idea what you were talking about, I assure you, I would not lie to you."

Logan rolled his eyes. "Yes, because that," he spat, "would be a first."

"What reason would I have to set Thomas Brittler against you?" Berkley insisted. "I wanted his daughter's money quite as much as you did."

He eyed Charlotte malevolently over Logan's shoulder. Logan glanced at her and was pleased to see that Charlotte was glowering right back. She was not silly enough to be cowed by his bullying.

"Well," said Logan, striding angrily around the room to clasp Charlotte's hand. The carpet let out little puffs of dust as he moved. "The joke is on you. I'm marrying Charlotte. I'm marrying her tomorrow, and there's not a thing that you can do to stop it."

"By all means," said his father, holding out his hands in a look of feigned innocence. "I've no reason to stop you. Although," he shot Logan a look of mock sympathy. "It is a pity about the merger. I suppose we'll have to battle on somehow."

Logan's blood boiled at the gibe and he started to turn back to his father. He wanted to shake him. To hurt him.

He wanted to shatter the expression of satisfaction he saw on his wrinkled, cunning face, but Charlotte held him back.

"What good would it do?" she asked him quietly.

Logan gave her hand a squeeze, and together, they left Drexel Manor through a side door.

❧

"Am I to take it that our courtship has officially ended?" asked Logan. He was riding beside Charlotte in the family's carriage, his arm snug around her shoulders.

"Hmm?" she said, looking up. She'd been gazing out of the window. Evidently, her mind was very distracted.

"You haven't managed to complain about my touching you since before we were engaged."

Charlotte looked up at him, frowning. Then she smiled. "I hadn't noticed," she said, giggling.

Logan laughed too.

"I suppose we aren't really courting anymore. We're about to be married."

"So," said Logan sliding his other hand over her knee, "You wouldn't mind if I kissed you?"

"Logan Drexel, you behave yourself," Charlotte said, slapping his hand away, but she ruined the effect slightly by continuing to grin.

Logan moved in closer to her, brushing his lips over her ear. "You must admit," he said, delicately. "I have behaved myself for quite a long time."

Charlotte wiggled in his arms. "That's enough of that, now," she said, giving him a light shove.

"Surely one kiss wouldn't hurt very much," pleaded Logan, settling back in his seat, and sighing.

Charlotte appeared to be considering him. "Oh, go on then," she said, smirking. "I suppose—."

Logan seized her face in his hands and pressed his lips to hers with fervor. She tasted of berries, somehow, inexplicably, and sweet pinot gris, and she was so warm in his arms.

He let his fingers trail lightly over her cheeks and twined one hand into her long, sweet-smelling hair. She was the only thing in his world. The only thing that mattered. The taste of her. The soft feel of her body as he pulled her against him.

They broke apart, gasping. Charlotte's face was crimson. She looked about ready to pass out.

"I was wrong," she said, fending him off with one arm as he made to pull her back into his embrace.

"One kiss could be disastrous to us both."

"Perhaps not," said Logan, grinning evilly. He tugged himself closer to her, and she came to him, trembling. Her dress had slipped down her shoulder, revealing a shock of pale, porcelain skin. Without thinking, Logan bent to press his warm lips to it. Charlotte gasped, and he knew that if he didn't pull away from her now, he would never be able to.

Logan didn't want to, but he released her with a growl, his heart thumping madly in his chest. He'd never been so full of painful, insatiable need. He sat back against the carriage seat and tucked Charlotte beneath his chin. For a long time, neither of them moved at all.

Charlotte was the first one to speak. "How will I get to the courthouse tomorrow?"

Logan shrugged. "I'll pick you up, of course."

She pulled away from him, looking scandalized. "You most certainly will not!"

"Why not? We're both heading to the same place, aren't we?"

"Yes, but you can't see me on the day of the wedding," she said exasperatedly.

Logan frowned. "What superstitious nonsense," he stated calmly. "I'll come and get you at eleven o'clock and—."

"No."

"Charlotte, don't be ridiculous."

"I'll hire a coach," she said firmly.

"Are you still determined that your parents won't be attending?" he asked. It saddened him to think that his wife falling out with the rest of her family was completely his fault.

"Not after the way Father treated you. No."

"He was defending his daughter."

"He never even gave you the chance to explain." Charlotte straightened her pins and spun the back of her head to him. "Is my hair alright?"

"It's fine," he said without glancing at it. He was still trying to make his point when the carriage pulled to a halt outside of the St. George. "Shall I join you for dinner?"

"Yes, alright," responded Charlotte, and with that, she gave him a swift kiss on the cheek, and slid out of the open carriage door. He felt the place where her mouth had touched him and knew the feel of her lips would linger long after she had gone.

But she was being stubborn. Angry she might be on his behalf, but Logan knew that Charlotte would deeply regret it if she allowed her family to miss her wedding day.

He stuck his head out the carriage window. "Four hundred and sixty-two, Lindbrock Place," he said to his driver. He had some explaining to do.

Chapter Fifteen

CHARLOTTE'S WEDDING DRESS WAS simple, white linen and lace. It flowed around her body in light waves, giving only the barest hint to her figure. She liked it quite a lot. She'd half expected Logan to try and collect her, so she wasn't surprised to see a carriage waiting for her when she stepped out of the hotel lobby. What did surprise her was that the man standing outside of the carriage was not her husband-to-be.

"Father?" she said, astounded.

Thomas Brittler approached his daughter, looking sheepish. "Hello, my dear," he said, holding out his arms. Charlotte ran to him. It was as if their argument of a few days ago had never happened. "Oh, my darling," he said, burying his face in her hair as he embraced her, "can you forgive me?"

Charlotte began to cry. "I already have," she said, and she was surprised to find that this was perfectly true. "How did you know where I was?"

Thomas Brittler cleared his throat. "Logan came to see me yesterday."

"He did?!"

"Yes, he did," said Thomas, and he looked very sheepish. "He told me the story of your engagement. He told me how you doubted him too. I must admit that I was rather proud to say I raised you to have a steady head on your shoulders."

"Of course, you did!" cried Charlotte, hugging him harder still.

"Thomas, Charlotte!" Charlotte looked around at the sound of her name to see her mother's head poking out of the waiting carriage. "You must hurry, or we'll be late!"

They weren't late. Noelle, Sarah, and her mother fussed over her in the carriage, and Charlotte found herself so deliriously happy, she didn't mind that she couldn't understand a word of their endless chatter. They pulled to a halt in front of the courthouse and Charlotte held tight to her father's arm as they walked across the threshold.

And then they were there, and Logan was standing, waiting for her at the end of a short aisle in front of the magistrate. And he looked more handsome than Charlotte had ever seen him, his smile nervous and excited and sheepish.

"I'm sorry," he whispered as she quietly traded her father's arm for his. "I couldn't let you marry without them here."

"Thank you," she whispered back, and feeling as though her heart would burst, she stepped forward with him to say her vows.

One week later

The keeper of the auction house was red-faced with exertion as he shouted for quiet from the raised platform. He beamed around at the assembly of Manhattan's wealthiest and it couldn't have been plainer that he was anticipating the biggest sale of his life.

"Ladies and gentlemen, I hope you all got the chance to review the collection in the entrance hall before the bidding starts."

There was a general mutter of ascent.

Charlotte was sitting beside her husband, scowling, with a glass of cold water in her hand. He had insisted, much to her irritation, that they attend today's sale, and as he had refused to tell her the reason—for she knew full-well that he didn't intend to buy any of the pieces—she was feeling rather grumpy that she had to be here at all.

"I'm just going to step out for some air," she whispered to Logan as many people began to take their seats.

"Please stay," he begged, taking her hand and giving it a gentle tug. "For me?" he asked sweetly.

Charlotte glared at him. "Oh, very well," she said, and she sat down in a huff and arranged her skirts around her ankles. Logan beamed at her. The auctioneer pounded his gavel, and the room gradually fell silent.

"Hello, Miss Brittler." Charlotte looked around at the whisper.

"Mr. Grimsby," she said enthusiastically, giving the man a friendly pat on the arm. "How are you? Haven't you heard, I'm Mrs. Drexel now." She grinned at Logan.

Mr. Grimsby's eyes widened to the size of saucers.

"I'm—."

"Quiet, please!" called the auctioneer from the front. They were about to start the bidding.

Charlotte held a finger to her lips, indicated that they could talk afterward, and turned to face the front of the room.

"As you all know," called the auctioneer, still beaming. "We're bidding on a very special collection today. As the painter still wishes to remain anonymous, we have christened these pieces Lady Red."

One by one, the paintings were brought in from the gallery and stood on the platform. There were six in all. Charlotte glanced at Logan who was smiling and looking very pleased about something. She raised her eyebrows at him, but he merely shook his head.

"We'll start with the painting furthest on my right and move down the line until the end."

At this, Mr. Grimsby, who was sitting just behind Charlotte, stood up.

"Will you not be selling them as a complete collection?!" he squawked, sounding outraged, and dabbing at his forehead with his yellowed handkerchief. "It's a terrible shame to divide such beautiful pieces. They should be kept together as a set!"

A small murmur ran through the crowd at this. Faces turned to look at Mr. Grimsby, who turned beet red with embarrassment and promptly sat back down again.

The auctioneer glared at him. "As I said, we will begin the bidding on each piece separately. Shall we get started then? We'll open the bidding at two hundred dollars."

And on it went. Charlotte never raised her paddle. She wished she could have because Lady Red was a fantastic collection. She wanted to own them very much, but they didn't have the funds. Again, she cast a sideways glance at her husband, who neither raised his paddle nor seemed to notice her looking.

"One thousand and five hundred dollars, going once, going twice, sold to Mr. Grimsby of Manhattan."

Charlotte started at the familiar name and looked behind her for Mr. Grimsby, but he was not looking at her. He was sweating worse than ever and truly looked in danger of being sick.

"That's wonderful, congratulations," she hissed.

Mr. Grimsby nodded.

The bidding started up again. Charlotte watched, astounded, as the bids grew higher and higher until finally,

Mr. Grimsby had purchased each and every one, his total climbing towards twelve thousand dollars. There was some very unappreciative muttering at this. It was clear that the rest of Manhattan's society rather resented being outbid on every piece.

"I would remind you," said the auctioneer, who was eyeing Mr. Grimsby suspiciously, "that once you have won the bid, the sale is final. You are obligated to pay, and there will be no returning the pieces to the auction house or to the artist."

"I'm well aware of that, thank you," Mr. Grimsby responded. He appeared to be in a rather sour mood. Charlotte couldn't think why. As far as she was aware, the Grimsby's had the money to spare.

"Well, Mr. Grimsby," said Logan, hopping up to wring the man's hand. "You got your wish! The collection will stay together, as you so rightly said it should."

Mr. Grimsby took his hand back from Logan, looking as though he had just sunk his arm up to the elbow in manure.

"I do not accept your congratulations, sir," he said, glaring at Logan with something remarkably close to hatred. "I know the kind of man you are."

Logan looked affronted, he raised his eyebrow at Mr. Grimsby. "I'm sorry if I have done something to...wait a moment." Understanding swept suddenly across Logan's face. He patted his coat pocket, frowning, and then he smiled blandly. "It was you, Mr. Grimsby."

"What about me?" Mr. Grimsby snapped, already turning away from Logan. Charlotte stared from one to the other of them, completely bemused.

"You stole the note from my pocket. You sent it to Mr. Brittler, didn't you?"

Charlotte's brow furrowed as she watched Mr. Grimsby sputter.

"I-I haven't the faintest idea what you're talking about," said Mr. Grimsby scathingly. "Now, if you don't mind, I'd like to pay for my new collection."

"Yes, of course," Logan sat back down.

"You really think it was him?" Charlotte asked.

"The night we were in the garden, don't you remember? He brought me my coat. I'd stuck the letter in my pocket."

"Of course," sighed Charlotte slapping her hand to her forehead. "But why would he..?"

"Look at him, Charlotte. Look at the way he fawns over you. He just spent twelve thousand dollars on a series of paintings that resemble you."

Charlotte felt her insides begin to boil. "How dare he!" she hissed, "what right did he have?"

"Just wait, dear, just wait."

Charlotte had stood up, outraged, and went to stalk after Mr. Grimsby. "Wait for what?" she growled as Logan grabbed her arm.

Logan, ridiculously, was grinning from ear to ear. "Just watch," he said. He nodded towards the raised platform.

As Mr. Grimsby scribbled down his signature for each of the pieces, the auctioneer's assistant ran up to the podium, clutching a seventh portrait covered with a golden cloth, and whispered into the auctioneer's ear.

"My assistant has just informed me that the artist has added a last minute piece to the collection," he shouted. His eyes found Logan questioningly, and Charlotte, confused, saw Logan give him a nod and a wink. Logan's knee was bouncing, as though he couldn't contain his excitement, and Charlotte was looking from her husband to the auctioneer, to the many canvases filled with the red-haired beauty. Understanding blossomed rapidly in her mind's eye and her mouth dropped open slowly.

She caught Logan watching her.

The crowd had resumed their seats, all mutters and excited whispers. Mr. Grimsby had looked around as he tore a check from his book and handed it to the auctioneer's assistant. "There's another?" he said excitedly.

"Yes, there is, sir. If you will resume your seat." The auctioneer gestured to the audience, who were all watching the veil on the next painting with bated breath.

"Mr. Cresswell, would you lift the covering?"

The auctioneer's assistant looked just as excited as everyone else did, but Charlotte couldn't suppress a sudden thrill of foreboding.

Logan was staring at her, and Charlotte was watching the veil, transfixed.

The gold cloth was pulled away, and the entire room let out an audible gasp. Charlotte felt the blood rush from her face as every single eye in the auction house found her and fixed her where she sat.

...It was her. The woman in the paintings, whose face had never been shown, she stared down at them all, wrapped in golden, flame-haired, incandescent beauty, with eyes as bright as emeralds.

Charlotte lifted a shaking hand to her lips as she gazed up at her husband. "Was it truly you? All along?" she whispered.

Logan's grin was telling. "How could it not be?" he asked her.

And then the room erupted. Men and women were throwing their paddles into the air so fast that the auctioneer hardly had time to call them out. "One thousand and seven hundred. Two thousand from Lady Grey. Two thousand and five from Mr. March. Three thousand from Johnathon Taylor. Four thousand. Five thousand! Six!"

On and on it went until finally, the auctioneer said, with his brow sweating madly. "Ten thousand and five hundred dollars going once, going twice! Sold to Mr. Hartley of Remmington Arms."

The entire room seemed to wither slightly, and Charlotte sat slumped in her seat, her eyes streaming with tears, as Logan mounted the podium to collect his dues. Heads turned and eyes followed him as he signed the check alongside Mr. Hartley, and then, smiling, he stepped up beside his painting to shake hands with him. Before he descended the stairs, he turned and gave the entire assembly a deep bow.

The applause started slowly at first, and then it grew into a tumultuous noise that echoed off the stone walls and filled Charlotte's ears with a heady ringing. Logan smiled as he approached her, and then, laughing and waving at his admirers, he led his wife out of the room. Past the empty gallery walls. Past the now-closed doorway that led to the auction house storage. Past a furious looking Mr. Grimsby, who—it appeared—had left the auction without bidding on the final piece.

They headed outside together, beaming and—in Charlotte's case—sobbing; and they held tight to one another as they climbed into their carriage and set off. Moving forward. Onward.

As Charlotte stared out the carriage window, her mind still grappling with the impossibility of her circumstances, she knew a blindingly sweet moment of happiness. Logan's fingers pressed into her own, and she looked up at him and shook her head.

"I should have known it was you," she whispered.

Logan was staring at her, and in his eyes, she seemed to sense a love that went beyond words, beyond thought, or passion. It went into her very soul, and lodged itself there, wrapping her heart in its warm embrace.

Her husband brought her fingers to his lips and pressed them to her knuckles. He snuggled in closely beside her, and they both turned to watch Manhattan trundle past the window.

When Logan began to hum, it was a few seconds before she recognized the tune.

There once was a lass who stole my heart. Diddly-diddly doo. There was once a lass who stole my heart, and my darling, Charlotte, 'twas you.

EPILOGUE

THE LONGEST MONTH IN Charlotte Drexel's life was drawing to a close. An unusually frigid Spring was fading into a balmy Summer, and the Drexel's mansion was a cold and unforgiving blot on the landscape behind her.

She was sitting in the gardens, as she so often did these days, with a book in her hand. It was a long time before she realized that the words on the pages were slipping through her mind without leaving the slightest trace of meaning in their wake.

Logan had left Manhattan on the fifth of May. Now May was falling into June, and Charlotte was feeling very much abandoned. She knew that she ought not to. Logan would return to her as soon as he was able, but her heart ached for him.

Logan's parents, Mr. and Mrs. Drexel, were not the pleasant sort. She had known this before she had married their son, but that did not make living alone with the pair of them any the more pleasant.

She sighed and slapped her book closed in her lap. The gold-embossed words on the front cover glared at her as they reflected the sunlight, and she flinched.

She registered the sounds of approaching footsteps with dismay. Mrs. Drexel had recently taken to berating Charlotte to join her for tea every afternoon, an occurrence that was neither amusing nor enjoyable, and one that she no longer had any desire to repeat.

"I'm afraid that I'm not very hungry just yet," she said before Mrs. Drexel could speak. "I think perhaps that I might take a ride in the park."

"Could I join you?" To Charlotte's surprise, the voice that had spoken did not belong to Mrs. Drexel. No.

As she spun around, her book tumbled off her lap with a plop, and Charlotte stood so suddenly that she nearly toppled over the chair on which she was sitting.

It was Logan, and his broad smile was the most welcoming thing she had ever imagined. Without pausing to think, Charlotte flung herself at her husband.

Logan began to laugh as his arms encircled her, his voice deep and warm and so delightfully essential. "So, have you missed me?" he asked playfully.

"Missed you?!" squeaked Charlotte. She drew back and slapped him on the shoulder. Judging by Logan's responding wince, she had hit him much harder than she had meant to. "Logan Drexel, if you ever leave me on my own with your parents again I promise, I will slaughter you."

Logan laughed harder still, then he gathered Charlotte's furious face into his hands and kissed her. It was as though cool, refreshing iced tea was sliding down her throat, cooling her boiling insides, and relaxing her exhausted muscles. As his lips moved over hers, she knew that the world had righted itself. Logan was home, and she was now wrapped securely in his warm embrace, precisely where she belonged.

They gripped one another tightly, swaying on the spot, their breath mingling in the warm air with the scent of roses.

At last, Charlotte pulled away.

"So," she whispered excitedly, "how did it go?"

Logan gripped her hand and led her over to the seat she had just abandoned. Just outside of the garden gate, they could hear the city traffic clip-clopping by. A carriage wheel squeaked on the unseen street beyond.

Logan was hesitating, staring at Charlotte's face as though he was drinking in the sight of her as much as she was him.

"Come on," she urged him. "Tell me."

Logan's lips curled in the corner. "It went...well..." he said slowly. "Stephen Harkness seemed rather impressed with the company's financial state."

"Was he now?" giggled Charlotte. "I suppose you didn't bother to tell him that the company's debts had only recently been equalized?"

"Actually," said Logan, now looking sheepish, "The subject did come up."

"Did it? What did he say?"

"Honestly?" said Logan, now examining a nearby rose bush with interest. "I think he was rather impressed with our dramatic recovery."

Charlotte grinned excitedly, running her fingers along Logan's knee to grip his hand. She couldn't seem to stop herself from touching him. "Soooo? Did it work then?"

"Not... exactly. Not like I'd hoped."

Charlotte's shoulders slumped. "So he didn't take it? The company?"

"No. He didn't take it." Logan didn't look as troubled by the idea as she had thought he would.

"Why ever not? I thought you said he was impressed!"

"He was," said Logan, exhaling sharply. He reached up and removed his hat, running the fingers of his left hand through his dark hair. "He refused to take over Drexel Industries. Instead, he offered me a partnership."

Charlotte stared at him. "A partnership?

"Standford Oil needs someone to aid in the running of the new branch in the Dakota Territory. The job fell to Harkness, but he has a wife and kids at home in Ohio. He doesn't want to stay there. They needed someone who understands the industry, who has experience managing a factory on shaky legs." Logan sat back. He was watching Charlotte, his expression tense. "Harkness' offer is this. That Standford Oil and Drexel Industries merge their resources. My grandfather's company will maintain its standing but will become a subsidiary of Standford Oil. In return, I will have to relocate to Bismarck, and maintain the new branch there until it is functioning well enough to stand on its own."

Charlotte's eyebrows flew up. "Relocate? To Bismarck?"

Logan nodded his head wearily.

Charlotte sat for a moment, only half-aware of Logan's thumb stroking over the skin on the back of her hand. Then she smiled.

Logan appeared a little shocked. "I didn't expect you to be very happy about the idea."

Charlotte's grin widened, and she suddenly threw back her head and laughed so loudly that a bluebird in a nearby tree took flight at the noise.

"What is it?" asked Logan, completely baffled by her reaction.

"If we're in Bismarck," giggled Charlotte, calming down. "I will never, ever have to have tea with your mother again."

And now Logan laughed, and at the same moment, they leaned towards one another. This time, when they kissed, the noise of the city fell away. Charlotte already felt as though she were flying away from Manhattan. She might have been on the wings of the bluebird, now fluttering off into the breeze. But she knew that wherever she went, whether in Manhattan, or in Bismarck, or even in some far off country... as long as Logan was beside her, she would be home.

The End

There's more to come! Stay up to date by signing up for
Josephine Blake's Newsletter
and recieve a FREE copy of *The Heart of Hope-A Brittler
Sisters Prequel.*

ABOUT THE AUTHOR

Josephine Blake is a *USA Today* Bestselling Author and an Award-Winning Graphic Designer. She enjoys a quiet life on a comfortable piece of property in her very own small-town in the Willamette Valley.

With over 20 published books in the romance genre, Josephine works hard to make sure her stories bring a little more love into this crazy world.

She and her husband spend most days chasing their little one around their farmhouse with thankful hearts.

Notable Works:

Josephine Blake's debut Historical Romance novel, *Dianna*, hit the shelves in August of 2016 and became a bestseller two years later. Her Gothic Historical Romance novel, *A Brush with Death*, followed suit later that year in

2018. Yours at Yuletide became her very first Contemporary Romance release in the winter of 2019.

Sign Up for her newsletter to stay up to date on every new release at www.awordfromjosephineblake.com.

ALSO BY JOSEPHINE BLAKE

The Brittler Sisters Series

Dianna

Little Rose

Charlotte

Sarah-Jane

Noelle

The Heart of Hope

The Brides of Adoration

Maid in the West

Cowboy, Take Me Away

The Arms of a Stranger

Nursing His Heart

JOSEPHINE BLAKE

Sweet Love of Mine
Brenden's Bookish Bride

❧

Love in Unity Springs
Yours at Yuletide
Second-Chance Santa
Mistletoe Miracles
Candy-Cane Kisses
Christmas in Unity Springs-Series Collection

❧

Standalones
Two Hearts, One Stone

❧

Multi-Author Projects
The ABC Mail Order Brides-Emeline's Exile

Charming Tales-Little Red
Silverpines Series-Wanted: Lawyer and Wanted: St. Nick

❧

Josephine Blake also Writes Gothic Victorian Romance under her middle name, Elizabeth.

Titles by Elizabeth Blake

The Hands of Fate Series
A Brush with Death
A Twist of Fortune
A String of Lies

❧

Standalones
Dark was the Night

www.ingramcontent.com/pod-product-compliance
Lightning Source LLC
Chambersburg PA
CBHW010331140726
47989CB00008BA/3040